THE VIRGINIA CITY BRIDE

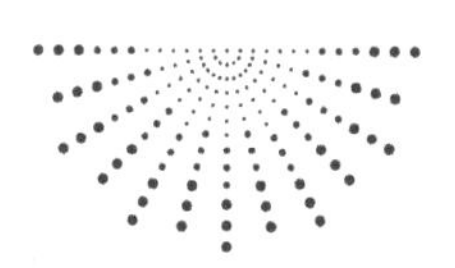

CYNTHIA WOOLF

Published by Firehouse Publishing
Woolf, Cynthia

CHAPTER ONE

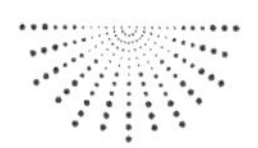

Hannibal, Missouri, July 22, 1862
The Riley home

Angelica Ellen Riley was thirty-years-old and starting over for the second time. This time alone. At least the first time she'd had Michael to share the adventure with. She was a doctor's wife and he had just started his own practice. That was in 1855.

She sat in the living room, looked around at the bare walls and sighed. She'd been twenty-three and so naïve. Michael always liked to tease her about her background growing up on a farm. But she was stubborn and strong minded. Those two characteristics had served her well when Michael was killed at the Battle of Rich Mountain, West Virginia on July 11, 1861, just four months after joining the Union army. She would never forget that date…the day her world came to an end.

A cannon ball made a direct hit on the operating tent killing him, the patient he was working on and the doctor that was assisting.

The colonel, who came to the door to tell her, assured her Michael didn't suffer.

She remembered he'd joined the army because they were in dire need of doctors. Michael wanted to do his part and serve his country. She was so proud of him but missed him more than she thought it possible to miss someone.

Now, that he was gone, she was leaving all that behind. All the savings she and Michael accumulated had kept her alive for the past year while she mourned. But the money was almost gone…time to move on. If she was careful, she had enough money to let her live independently for another year, but she wanted a family, and she didn't want to work for pennies, when the money was gone, just to survive.

Her choices were limited, but she wanted a husband and children above all else, so she had visited Brides for the West. a mail-order bride agency. She signed up on the spot. Finding a husband would give her the stability and security she sought as well.

A week later a girl arrived from the agency. "Mrs. Ward wants you right away. Come with me back to the agency."

When she arrived, Mrs. Ward, an older woman in

her mid-to-fifties, with steel gray hair, practically leapt from her chair, waving a letter in her hand.

"Angelica, this just came in. All I know of the man is what is in his letter. He seems educated, his letter is written beautifully. He sent money for the agency fees and for the bride's travel expenses. He's the marshal in Virginia City, Nevada Territory. Would you be interested in someone like him?"

She read his letter. He sounded like her, ready to raise a family. He'd never been married. Angelica looked over the top of the letter. "I accept. When can I leave?"

"As soon as you like." Mrs. Ward smiled. "I can't believe this came in and fit you so perfectly. You're both in your thirties, want children and want to be married right away." She bustled back around the desk and sat in her leather chair. "You'll need to arrange shipping of your trunks, if you have any. Don't take more than you can carry—two carpetbags at the very most, and even at that be prepared to lose one. Though the stagecoach carries passengers, it is mainly for carrying mail. The trip won't be comfortable by any stretch of the imagination."

She handed Angelica an envelope. "Here is the two-hundred dollars for the stage from St. Joseph to Virginia City and for the train from here to St. Joseph. The marshal seemed to be very certain we'd find someone because he sent the money with the letter."

"I think that is very trusting of him. You must have a

great reputation for him to send the money before he has a match."

"We do have a fine reputation. Our clients trust us with their futures and often, when they are so far away, they also trust us with their money, so they can get a wife as quickly as possible."

"Should I write him a letter, accepting his proposition?"

"Yes, I believe you should. I'll mail it right away and it should reach Virginia City before you do. How long before you'll be leaving?"

"I am almost ready. No more than two or three days. I have to be out of the house in four days, so I'll leave for Virginia City before that."

"Then you'd better write that letter quickly so I can get it on the mail train immediately."

Angelica sat and wrote a letter to her future husband.

Marshal Winslow, I am Angelica Riley. I wish to have a family as I understand you do as well and I accept your proposition.

I will be arriving by stagecoach on approximately August 20, 1862 assuming all goes well with the journey.

I am a widow, my late husband, Michael, died in the war.

I look forward to meeting you and beginning our life together.

Angelica Riley

Her desire was a husband and children. She'd never love anyone other than Michael, but he would understand her need to move on and find someone to give her the family she wanted. Once she left the agency she arranged for her trunks to be forwarded to the marshal. The furniture had been sold with the house, which she thought unusual, but was grateful for it, too. It meant she'd had a bed to sleep in until she left for Virginia City.

On July 24, 1862, Angelica left Hannibal and traveled by train to St. Joseph where she picked up the stagecoach to Virginia City. The stagecoach trip was supposed to take twenty-five days. Thank goodness she'd shipped her trunks ahead of her and kept only two carpet bags with her. But even at that, she might be limited to what she had with her for some time, if the freight didn't make it through.

She'd sewn most of her money, almost two hundred and fifty dollars, into the lining of the blue bag. That piece of luggage also had her wedding dress and petticoats. The green bag held two changes of clothing, shoes, a spare corset and bloomers.

She'd always return to the coach early so she got a window seat. Then she spent her time gazing out at the changing countryside, amazed by the different types of country she went through. The date was August nineteenth and most of the land was still green. Lush fields full of corn just waiting to be harvested. Acres and acres of sunflowers grew as far as the eye could see.

The prairie was covered in tall grass.

Buffalo herds thundered across the land, halting the stagecoach's progress for hours.

She took this time to read while the coach wasn't moving. She'd found a book about the expansion of the west and what rough and tumble place it was. The book said no woman was safe there because there were so many men.

Virginia City's populace of mostly men spent their time, when they weren't working, drinking and supporting the saloons and also all the other business' that come with a town. The mercantiles, bakeries, butchers. The population was around four thousand and growing by leaps and bounds because of the discovery of silver. The largest of the silver finds was called the Comstock Lode and employed hundreds of men.

Virginia City sounded like a bustling town. Not as big as Hannibal, but not really small either.

They had to cross the Rocky Mountains and Angelica was amazed at their heights. Snow covered the tallest peaks even in August. The road they traveled went high into the mountains before coming down the other side. She was very glad to be down and had closed her eyes for most of the way because it was so high and steep.

She spent most of the time after they passed the mountains, just thankful to be out of them. When the shotgun rider announced the next stop she could almost breathe again.

In Carson City, the stage stopped in front of the hotel. She noticed in every town they stopped in they pulled up in front of a hotel, if there was one. The further she got away from Missouri, the more stares she got from men.

She'd kept her clothes handy incase she could bathe or change clothes. Neither of which she could so far on the stagecoach trip to Nevada Territory, since there was no privacy at any of the way stations. She'd kept forty dollars out for food and hoped to find somewhere to bathe during the journey, but that had proved to be for naught.

The seat in the stage was barely more than a plank of wood upholstered with heavy broadcloth.

She got out to stretch her legs and relieve her sore backside and almost caused a mob to form. Men gathered around her. In Carson City, every person she saw was a man and many of them would stand tall and strut in front of her.

A short, old man with long gray hair, under a floppy hat, approached her. "Hi, there missy."

Angelica looked down at him nodded her head once. "Sir."

"How'd ya like to marry me?" He sidled up next to her and whispered. "I'm rich." Then he waggled his eyebrows.

She stepped away from him. "Um, no thank you."

He walked away.

Another man took his place with the same question.

She gave him the same answer. Then she noticed a line of men forming. She walked to the stairs to the hotel behind her and stepped up several so she could see and be seen by the crowd of men.

"Gentlemen, please, get on about your business. I'm not marrying any of you."

The line busted up with many grumbles.

While standing there, a man with blond hair and a handlebar mustache decided to approach her. He wasn't like the other men. He was clean and well dressed.

"Excuse me, miss, are you staying here in Carson City?" He rolled his mustache between his fingers. "Forgive me for not introducing myself. I'm Clay Stockton."

She nodded. "Angelica Riley, and no, Mr. Stockton, I'm not staying in Carson City. I'm meeting my fiancé in Virginia City."

He frowned. "Oh, how sad for me. Perhaps I know him. I'm from there."

Angelica perked up. "Then you probably do. I'm marrying Marshal Winslow, who should be expecting me. I'm a mail-order bride you see and I should have arrived two days ago." She ran her hand over her skirt as she did at every stop where she could get out and walk. Most times the stage just changed the team of horses which took less than ten minutes and passengers were only out long enough to relieve themselves.

"Winslow? Jared Winslow?"

She saw his hands fist at his sides and lifted her brows. “Yes, do you know him?”

His mouth formed a thin line and his eyes narrowed, his brows nearly came together above them. “Yes, I know him. You’d be better off marrying me.” He smiled and rolled his mustache again. “As a matter of fact, why don’t you marry me? I’m rich and handsome, or so I’m told and you’ve already met me.”

Her stomach turned, she was thoroughly repulsed by this man and his sallow complexion and bloodshot eyes. He obviously liked to drink and she had no time for drinkers. She shook her head. “I don’t think so. I’m promised to Marshal Winslow and I always keep my promises.”

“I’m taking the stage to Virginia City as well. Perhaps I can convince you to see things my way. You see I never lose. You will be mine.”

She lifted her chin. “You’ll lose this time for I have no intention of not marrying Marshall Winslow or ever marrying you.”

Mr. Stockton tied his horse to the back of the stage, climbed inside and sat across from her.

They reached Virginia City later that day. The stage trip had been twenty-seven days long due to buffalo herds, bad weather, a broken wheel and missing horses. The missing horses were the worst of it. In order to make the next station with tired horses, the stage had to go slow. If they didn’t the animals might have died and the passengers might have followed.

The last sixteen miles from Carson City to Virginia City seemed longer than the full twenty-seven days of the stagecoach journey even though according to her pin watch, the trip had taken more than three hours. Clay Stockton spoke nonstop and did everything to try to convince her to marry him. He told her how rich he was, how he would be able to keep her in luxury. Quite scandalously he said he could keep her satisfied in the bedroom. After that, she stopped listening and looked out the window while he went on and on about what he could do for her.

When they reached Virginia City, the stage again stopped in front of the hotel. The stagecoach driver, Zeke Murdoch, came around to help her down from the coach..

"Thank you, Mr. Murdoch." She placed her hand in his and navigated the tiny steps out of the stagecoach.

"You're very welcome, Mrs. Riley. Anytime you want to ride this stage, me and Ben will be happy to have you."

She tilted her head and smiled. "Ah, that's so sweet. I'll keep your offer in mind."

"Have a great life, Mrs. Riley."

"You as well, Mr. Murdoch."

Ben handed her the two carpetbags, one had been under her feet and the other on her lap during most of the journey. "There you are, Mrs. Riley. Like Zeke says, we'd be happy to have you again on our stage. A lovelier person I ain't never met."

"Why thank you, Mr. Bullock. I appreciate the compliment."

Clay Stockton came forward. "Here, I'll take those bags for you." He picked up the bags.

"Fine. You can carry them up the steps and set them on the boardwalk in front of the Virginia City Hotel."

Now that he'd picked up the bags, he didn't really have any choice and carried the bags up the stairs, dropped the bags and kept walking into the hotel.

Angelica picked up her bags and carried them out of the way. The three story building was painted a soft yellow with dark brown shutters on the windows of the main floor. The front double doors were open and the lobby looked very inviting with an Oriental rug in front of the desk. She knew from having been inside other hotels, that behind the desk was a board with a cubby for each room. The cubby's held the room key and if the room was occupied they would hold any message for the occupant of the room.

Angelica was so tempted to get a room and a bath.

"Mrs. Riley?"

A man's deep voice startled her from her reverie. She turned to face a man with dark brown hair on the longish side, with a perfectly groomed mustache—*not a handlebar style, thank God*—and the bluest eyes she'd ever seen. He was tall, at least six feet, towering a good head over her. *Oh, please let him be Marshal Winslow.*

"Yes, I'm Angelica Riley. Who might you be?"

"I'm Jared Winslow." He held out his hand.

She released the breath she held, smiled and shook his hand. "Very nice to meet you, Mr. Winslow."

"I'm happy to make your acquaintance, too. I've been checking for the stage every day for the past week. We just never know what kind of time they'll make. The buffalo herds have stopped them for more than a day on several occasions."

"Out of my way, Winslow." Clay Stockton pushed his way between Angelica and Jared, knocking her off balance.

Jared grabbed Stockton by the coat lapels. "Apologize to the lady, Stockton."

He looked Angelica up and down. "I don't see any lady, just another whore—"

Angelica gasped. *I've never been called anything before much less a whore. Michael would roll over in his grave at such a name being used to describe me.*

Jared's fist shot out so fast, Angelica almost didn't see it. She widened her eyes and her eyebrows went skyward. "Oh, my."

"You will apologize to my fiancée. Now."

Stockton wiped the blood away from his mouth. He looked first at Angelica and then at Jared. "Forgive me. You two deserve each other." He straightened his jacket and walked down the street.

Jared removed his hat. Dark brown hair lay flat against his head where his hat had been. "I'm sorry that happened."

"It's all right. Being in the coach with him was

worse than being stopped for hours by a broken wheel in the middle of the desert."

He laughed.

Jared Winslow had a great smile with dimples on both sides of his mouth and straight, white teeth, under his mustache. Angelica liked it very much.

She stared.

Jared stopped laughing, but his mouth turned up a bit on one side showing his remaining mirth. "Forgive me. I haven't met anyone who said exactly what I think of Stockton."

Angelica looked down at her hands, before looking back up into those deep blue eyes. . "I guess I'm a little punchy from the trip and being stuck and badgered by Clay Stockton for more than three hours."

He chuckled. "You're fine. I'd be more than punchy enduring that trip and then ending it with Stockton."

She changed the subject. "Have my trunks arrived yet?"

"Yes, they came a week ago. That was another reason I checked every stage that arrived. I knew you had to be coming soon if your trunks were here."

She nodded. "That makes sense." Angelica clasped her hands in front of her. "What happens now? I'd really like to clean up before we do anything else."

He ran a hand behind his neck. "I'd take you to my house and let you have a bath, but coming alone to my home's probably not proper, much less taking a bath there."

Eyes wide, she stared up at him. "Who cares about proper? We're about to be married and if anyone found out about it, we'd just be forced to marry anyway. And since we are about to do that, I'd like a bath first." *Her skin and scalp itched, her hair was greasy, her clothes dirty and wrinkled. What must he think of her?*

Nodding, he picked up her bags with one hand and held out his other arm.

She put her hand in the crook of his elbow.

"Thank you. I appreciate a bath more than you can imagine."

"Oh, I think I can imagine it. I've taken that trip myself. It is pretty awful."

He turned them to his right and away from the rest of the town.

"You live outside of town? I'm surprised the town fathers would allow that."

"Oh, they don't like it, but I refused the tiny, crappy house next to the jail they offered me."

Her eyes widened again at the word *crappy*. She guessed she'd have to get used to the more colorful language used in the west.

"I built my home with the money I had saved for a house in Chicago. Since houses are much more expensive there, I was able to build a nice house here. And the city fathers don't have to keep it up. They just pay me each month for living expenses they would have paid me for the other house."

He turned right at the end to the boardwalk and they

kept walking toward a two-story, brick and stone house with dark green shutters.

A white picket fence surrounded the front yard and as they got closer she saw a flower garden on each side of the path to the house.

Jared stopped just outside the fence. "Well, what do you think of your new home?"

"So far, I like it very much. Is the inside as nice?"

He jerked back his head. "You think I would bring my bride to a wreck of a house?"

She lifted her brows. "I don't know you well enough to know if you would or not."

He chuckled. "Touché."

"Well, are you taking me inside? Or do we simply stand here and admire it?"

He smiled and opened the gate.

A path paved with flat, red flagstone led them through the flower garden to the front porch stairs.

"This front yard is lovely. You've done a very nice job out here."

"Thank you. I try. And I love working in the dirt, so it was a pleasure, not a chore."

"I know nothing about gardening…you'll have to teach me. Now, however, I really want that bath."

"Of course, come in." He took a key from his vest pocket and set it to the lock. Then he opened the door wide.

To her right, as she entered, Angelica saw a lovely

living room. Directly in front of her were the stairs to the second floor.

Jared closed the door and headed left, down a long hall.

She passed several doors and an open archway through which was the dining room.

Entering the kitchen, she almost squealed in delight. The room was a cook and bakers dream. On her right stood a small—compared to the dining room—table and six chairs. Beyond that, toward the icebox, stood a wonderful four burner stove with blue porcelain doors on the oven, firebox, and warming shelf.

Next was the four-door icebox, then a long counter with drawers and cupboards below and above it. Across from her was the large sink with a pump on the right side and a window above it looking out into the back-yard, where she saw a clothesline.

More counter, cupboards and drawers were between the sink and the back door.

On the wall to her left were pegs holding coats and a hat.

She hurried over to the stove and ran her fingers over the door on the warming shelf, then turned around with a wide smile. "This is wonderful. I couldn't ask for a nicer kitchen."

Jared stood with his thumbs in his pockets and rocked back on his heels. "I'm happy you think so. I built it with you in mind. Not you specifically, but with my wife in mind."

"I'd say you did very well." Her home in Missouri hadn't been as nice. The room was much smaller with only room for a round table and four chairs, though they only had two, seeing that they didn't entertain. The table they had folded down on the sides and so took even less room. She had a two-burner stove, a two-door icebox and fewer cupboards and drawers and counter space.

"Thanks. Do you want to see the rest of the house while the water heats?"

"Very much."

"Let me get the buckets on the stove." He built up the fire in the firebox.

While he did that, Angelica filled up one bucket and started on the other.

"Thank you for helping, but you shouldn't have to work on your wedding day." He finished filling the bucket.

She put her hands on her hips. "Why not? You are. We should share things and help each other as much as possible."

"Okay. I agree." He took the second full bucket and put it on the stove next to the first one. "Let me show you the rest of the house." He grabbed her hand and pulled her after him back into the hall.

"Along this hall is the dining room, which you saw coming in. Across from that is my office. I do a lot of my paperwork here at home. I'll do even more of it now, so I'm not away from you more than I have to be." He kept walking into the living room where he stopped.

Her face heated and came to points in her cheeks. "That's kind of you." *I won't have any more lonely nights in the house alone, in the bed alone. Never again will I have to endure...now I can live.*

He turned toward her and shook his head. "Nothing kind about it. Purely selfish on my part. I could look at you all day long. You're a very beautiful woman, Angel. I hope you don't mind. Angel seems to fit you."

"Now you're being crazy. I'm about as far as you can get from being an angel."

"I disagree. You're my angel."

She laughed. "Well, if it makes you happy, Angel it is."

"It does and you are."

Angelica rolled her eyes and laughed. "Just show me the rest of the house."

He grinned. "Upstairs are the bedrooms. I built four good sized rooms." He took her hand and again, pulled her after him up the stairs. "Here is the first room."

She poked her head inside. It was huge.

The room across the hall was the same way. "Have you thought of making these two rooms smaller? Especially the one next to our room. It could be a nursery."

He lifted a brow. "Ah, a woman who thinks ahead. I like that. A nursery it is. I'll building the wall next week after work."

Jared walked on to the last room on the right.

It, too, was quite large. This was the master bedroom. The bed, oversized to fit Jared's tall body, was in a carved wood frame with a forest scene of trees, deer, rabbits, bear and some sort of big cat. The bed, bureau with mirror, dresser, and commode were all of a dark wood.

"The furnishings are lovely, but I'm not familiar with the type of wood used."

"It's cherry wood. I had the bed made back east in Chicago and shipped here."

She ran her fingers over the footboard. "Well, I like it."

"I'm glad. Uh, the water is probably warm enough for a bath, if you're ready."

She sighed. "Oh, I'm ready…so much more than ready."

Yes, I'm ready for a bath, but am I ready to be married again? And to this man? He makes me laugh. I've laughed more today than I have in the last year. But marriage is so much more than laughter, can we really make a good marriage and if we're very lucky...good parents?

CHAPTER TWO

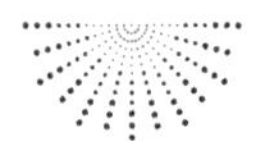

They went back to the kitchen.

Jared brought in the long metal tub from the porch out back. "One of these days I'll put in a real bathing room."

"A bathing room would be lovely." She looked at the wall the stove was on and noticed two doors. "Do you have two pantries?"

He chuckled. "That would be a bit too much. No, the right most door leads to a bedroom for the cook and housekeeper when we hire one and the other door is the pantry."

"Cook and housekeeper? How do you afford all this?" She waved her arm in a wide circle.

"I made good money as a Pinkerton Agent and then invested wisely. When I came here, I cashed everything in and have used part of it to buy the land and build this house."

"That's wonderful. As you know, I'm a widow and I had to sell our house and unfortunately, after all was said and done, I only had around three-hundred-fifty dollars left."

"Is that when you decided to become a mail-order bride?"

"I did, but this conversation can wait until I bathe. The water is hot, the tub is here and you were just leaving, were you not?"

He laughed. "I guess I know when I'm not wanted. After we get married, I'll wash your back for you and converse with you while you bathe."

"Well, for now, how about we fill that tub, and I'll get ready to be married?"

"I'll leave you to it."

She stood. "Thank you. I'll come out into the living room when I'm done."

He turned to leave.

Angelica stopped him with a hand on his arm. "Thank you for being a gentleman about this bath. I appreciate it very much. Oh, I need two towels and a washcloth. I have my soap in my bag."

He covered her hand with his. "Of course. I respect you and I would never have you believe the worst of me, especially in the beginning of our relationship." He grinned and tilted his head toward the tub. "But after we're married, I just might join you in that tub. But now, I'll just get you the towels you need."

She laughed. "This tub is too small for two fully grown adults."

He waggled his brows. "Then I'll have to buy a bigger one."

Angelica shook her head and pointed toward the door. "Get out of here," She moved her arm and pointed toward the stove. "Before I throw that bucket of water on you and you're the one who needs the towels."

He held up his hands. "I'm leaving. I'm leaving." Jared walked out but chuckled all the way.

Jared returned quickly with the towels. "Here you go. I'll set them next to the tub."

"Thank you."

"You're welcome." He left the room.

Angelica poured one and one half of the buckets into the tub, then filled them with cold water and added that, too. The water was now warm. She reserved half a bucket of the hot water for rinsing her hair. She added cold water to the bucket until the contents were just hot enough to be warm by the time her bath was done.

She undressed and her corset stuck to the sores it had caused. Angelica climbed into the warm water and a long sigh escaped her. She leaned back against the tub. The corset sores on her back and under her breasts, hurt like the dickens, but she knew they had to be cleaned, and so she waited until the pain subsided before sitting up and cleaning herself. She washed her hair last, thank goodness. It was full of dust, and she had to lather it twice to get it clean. Then she lay back and rinsed most of the suds out before using the remaining water to finish the job.

After she'd dried off, pinned up her wet hair into a bun at her neck before she opened her carpetbag and pulled out her wedding dress. She shook it out and donned the dress. She'd made it years ago when she was engaged to Michael. But on the spur of the moment, when they were picnicking they'd run away and gotten married, so she had never had an opportunity to wear it…until now. Without a mirror, she could only guess how she looked. The light pink dress was off the shoulder with small poufy sleeves. She smoothed the skirt as much as possible and hoped it was good enough.

The bodice was fitted and boned so no corset was necessary, but it still pressed against her sores. If I put up with the corset for twenty-seven days, I can put up with the boning in the gown for a few hours.

The garment went down to her waist except for a deep vee that extended six inches lower in front. The skirt was so full, she had thought it might be too much for her carpet bag, but she'd managed to put the petticoats and the dress's matching wrap inside. She had to wear two petticoats to achieve the fullness she wanted.

She entered the living room and as Jared shifted his gaze to her from the window, she knew she blushed.

Jared's jaw dropped and his mouth opened. "You take my breath away, Angel."

"I'm glad you like it. It was supposed to be my wedding dress to Michael but we ran away to be married and I was in one of my day dresses. I wasn't apprised that we would be getting married."

Angelica laughed quietly at the memory. "He was too anxious to be married to wait three months for the wedding, which my mother had planned down to the last detail. She was none to happy, I can tell you."

Jared's eyelids closed slightly and his nostrils flared. "I understand what he was thinking. I can barely wait until we walk to the preacher's house. Every woman we pass will be jealous of you for looking so stunning. Every man we pass will be jealous of me because I have you on my arm."

So much time had passed since he complimented her, she felt a secret thrill at his words. "That's very kind of you to say, but I think you grossly overestimate our effect on other people."

He shook his head and walked up to her, where he held out his arm.

She placed her hand through the crook in his elbow. "I want you to know, you look rather splendid in your suit."

"Thank you, I thought I should change. I didn't want to get married in my work clothes. I may be the marshal and I always wear my badge." He opened his coat to show her the badge pinned to his vest. "But that doesn't mean I won't dress for the occasion."

"Shall we go see the preacher? What is his name? I hate to just call him *the preacher*."

"His name is Virgil Moynihan. Everyone just calls him Reverend Verd, which is a nickname for Virgil."

"Very well, let's go see Reverend Verd and get this marriage started because so far, if we don't get married, my reputation is ruined."

He laid a hand over hers and squeezed lightly. "I would never let that happen."

"I'm very glad to hear my reputation is safe with you."

They walked past the mercantile, butcher, bakery and hardware store. Most of the buildings were made of brick and stone, like Jared's home. "I'm surprised at the use of brick and stone in all the buildings, especially your…our…home."

Virginia City is prone to fire and if we don't want to rebuild all the time, we needed to build them this way."

Finally, they passed the church on the way to the house directly next door

The preacher's home was an average size, single story wooden structure painted white with light blue shutters. A well-kept garden was on either side of the path to the front door. The house didn't have a front porch, but she did get a glimpse of one on the back. Maybe the builders didn't want the preacher to have to watch the comings and goings of his flock outside of church.

Jared knocked on the door.

Angelica's stomach flipped over. Despite her

bravado, she was terrified. Until they were actually married, she probably would feel that way.

The door opened and a woman with blonde hair answered. "Hello, Jared. I can see by your lovely lady's clothes that you two are here to get married. Let me get Verd for you, but first come inside and make yourselves at home."

"Thank you, Gladys. I appreciate it."

Jared waved an arm for Angelica to enter first.

Once they were both inside, Gladys closed the door. "You two have a seat and I'll be right back." She left through a door to Angelica's left.

They had entered into the living room. It was lovely, if sparsely decorated. The room was painted a light green, graced by a green brocade sofa and solid green chairs in the Queen Anne style. A low coffee table sat in front of the sofa with end tables between the sofa and the chairs. All three faced the rock fireplace. On the wall behind the sofa were bookshelves about half-full of books.

Jared squeezed her hand. "Nervous?"

She let out a short breath. "Yes and you? Are you nervous, too?"

"I've never been married before, so this event is all new to me. That would make anyone nervous."

Mrs. Moynihan emerged from what Angelica thought might be the kitchen. She was with two men. One was older and barrel-chested with dark hair, though he had lost most of the hair on top of his head. He was tall, matching Jared in height. The younger man was also tall, but much leaner than the older man, who looked to be his father.

"Jared. So good to see you. This must be your bride-to-be." The preacher turned to Angelica and clasped her hand between both of his. "It's so nice to meet you."

He didn't so much shake her hand as lightly squeeze it. Angelica smiled. She already liked him. "I'm pleased to meet you, too, Reverend Verd."

"Ah, I see Jared already told you my nickname. I do like it. Virgil is so formal and what my mother called me when I was in trouble." He laughed.

The sound was so deep it reverberated within her.

"This young man," he clapped the man on the back. "Is our son, Daniel. He's here with his wife and our four grandchildren, who are currently out shopping. Shall we get this wedding started?"

"Yes, sir," said Angelica.

"Yes, Reverend Verd," said Jared at the same time.

"Good. I'll stand in front of the fireplace and you two behind the sofa, with Gladys and Daniel."

Gladys stood to Angelica's left.

Daniel to Jared's right.

"Good," boomed the reverend. "Dearly beloved, we are gathered here in front of God and these witnesses, to unite this man and this woman in holy matrimony. Do you Jared, uh—"

"James," said Jared.

"Mine is Megan, Reverend," said Angelica.

"Good. Good." The reverend angled toward Jared. "Do you, Jared James Winslow, take this woman, Angelica Megan Riley, to be your lawfully wedded wife? To have and to hold, in sickness and in health, for richer and for poorer, and to keep yourself only unto her, as long as you both shall live?"

"I do." Jared's words were loud and clear. He reached over and took Angelica's hand in his, squeezing it ever so slightly.

"Very well." Reverend Verd turned toward Angelica. "Do you Angelica Megan Riley take this man, Jared James Winslow, to be your lawfully wedded husband? To have and to hold, in sickness and in health, for richer and for poorer, to honor and obey him and keep yourself only unto him, for as long as you both shall live?"

"I do." She squeezed Jared's hand, as he'd done hers.

"Then by the power vested in me by the Lord God Almighty and the city of Virginia City and the Nevada Territory, I now pronounce you man and wife. You may kiss your bride."

Angelica turned toward Jared, glanced up and smiled before closing her eyes.

"Open your eyes, Angel. I want to look into those gorgeous, brandy-brown eyes when I kiss you."

She opened her eyes and was filled with excitement. Her future was assured with a stable man. She felt safe for the first time since Michael's death

He captured her lips with his, kissing her deeply,

then his hands came up and cupped her face, caressing her, while they kissed.

When he pulled back, she followed him, forgetting where they were…forgetting everything but his talented lips.

She'd never been kissed like that. Even Michael, who she'd loved dearly, never kissed her so thoroughly she felt like he touched her soul, as Jared did.

Jared smiled and touched the tip of her nose with a finger. Then he winked.

She raised her eyebrows and blinked several times. What in the heck did that mean? Jared was an unusual man. He liked to tease her, which she found disconcerting since they didn't know each other yet.

Jared turned to the reverend. "How much do I owe you, Verd?"

"Two dollars will do."

Jared pulled a five-dollar gold piece from his pocket. "Yes, but five will do better. Take Gladys and the kids out to eat. It's an occasion. I just got married."

She was glad he was a generous man especially to the preacher. Angelica doubted a marshal made a lot of money.

He turned back to Angelica. "Come on, Angel. Let's go home."

"All right, but it's early. Do you have food for dinner?"

"We'll go out. I don't want you cooking on your wedding day."

She lowered her chin and gazed up through her lashes. She was lucky she'd been blessed with long, dark eyelashes. "What do you want me to do on my wedding day?" she whispered.

He laughed. "Not what you're thinking, my lovely wife…well, not entirely what you're thinking. Let's get our marriage certificate and be on our way."

Verd scribbled on a certificate with a gold seal and handed the document to Jared.

He shoved it into the inside pocket of his suit coat. "Thank you for marrying us. Goodbye all."

She turned to the reverend and his family. "Yes, thank you very much. I know we'll be seeing more of each other."

The reverend nodded. "Hopefully at church."

Jared pulled her away before she could answer. Not that she could have answered anyway, she didn't know what religion Jared practiced or if he was religious at all.

"Jared, what religion are you? Or do you not practice?

"I don't go to church very often. My duties usually keep me busy. I do the rounds so my deputies can worship with their families."

"Do you mind if I go alone?"

"Not at all. Go as often as you wish."

"Thank you."

They walked back down the boardwalk on the opposite side of the street that they had taken to the church.

This side had The Red Garter saloon, a blacksmith, and the doctor's office. She wasn't used to passing a saloon to do her shopping and kept her head high, her eyes straight ahead when they passed The Red Garter.

"Hey, Marshal, you finally get that lassie you sent for?" asked a big, man with red hair and beard.

"I did, Robert, and she's a beaut."

Robert appeared to be a friend of Jared's.

"Aye, I can see that, I'm not blind. Pleased to meet ye, Mrs. Winslow."

Angelica ducked her head a bit, pleased the man found her attractive. She'd received more compliments in this day than she'd received in the five years she was married to Michael. He never seemed to notice when she wore a new dress or styled her hair a different way. This was nice. And to be called Mrs. Winslow brought home the fact she was safe and secure. "And you, Mr…uh."

"It's no mister, I be just Robert. Robert MacGregor, from Scotland. If you need anything, you just give Robert a holler and he'll help ye."

She loved the burr to his speech. "Thank you, Mr. MacGregor, I mean Robert."

He laughed. "It's fine, Mrs. Winslow."

"I'm Angelica." She held out her hand.

Robert's hand engulfed hers as he shook it. "Nice to meet you…Angelica."

Jared took her other hand and started down the boardwalk. "Got to get going. See you later, Robert."

They were stopped again by another man. This one was older and balding.

"Jared. I just had to see your bride." He turned to Angelica. "I'm Phinneas Jones. I run the tobacco shop. I'm pleased to meet you." He held out his hand.

Angelica shook it. "Nice to meet you, too, Mr. Jones or is it Phinneas?"

He chuckled. "It's Phinneas. We don't stand on ceremony here. Everyone is known by their first name."

"Well, then, I'm Angelica."

"I must get back to my shop, but I enjoyed meeting you, Angelica."

She smiled and turned to Jared. "You appear to have several friends here in town."

"I do. For the most part these are all good people and if you treat them right, they will you, too."

"That's very good to know. I noticed in Carson City and here in Virginia City as well, that there are very few women. Why is that?"

"Most of these men are miners. They left their families back home and came here alone to find silver and make them rich. That rarely happens though. Most of them make enough a day to buy food or drink and shelter. Some of them not even that and they live on the streets. In many ways it's very sad."

"I see. I'll remember that."

"Okay let's go home before we meet anyone else." He took her hand and started walking.

Angelica had to run to keep up. "Stop. Jared. Stop."

She pulled her hand free of his and stopped, putting one hand on her hip and the other to her throat while she caught her breath. "Slow down, Jared, please. We'll get there in plenty of time without you running."

He looked around.

He appeared to be searching for someone.

"I'm afraid I've given you the wrong impression. I want you home and safe. That's all."

She put both hands on her hips, and her wrap fell to her waist. Angelica pushed it up her arms until it hung like a scarf around her neck. "Why wouldn't I be safe on the street? Everyone we've met has been very nice. We weren't in this kind of hurry to get to the preacher's, so why now?"

He ran a hand behind his neck and put the other in his pocket, while he looked down at his boots. "You're right, I need to slow down. I want us to be seen together and especially with you in your wedding dress."

"Why? I don't understand."

"I wanted Clay Stockton to see us. He's—"

Angelica's head jerked up "I met him on the stage. He got on the stage in Carson City and tried to get me to marry him instead of you. Since I'd never met you, I might have been tempted if not for his obvious love of the bottle."

"How did you know that he likes to drink too much? He rarely drinks except in town, never when traveling."

"His sallow complexion and bloodshot eyes give him away. My father was a drinker and looked the same way." She stepped over to Jared and took his arm. "You're right. We should take this conversation inside, but at a walk, not a run."

He chuckled. "All right." Jared patted her hand. "A walk, it is."

I also want Clay Stockton to see me in my wedding dress, especially coming from the preacher's home. Maybe he'll leave me alone. What about Clay Stockton has Jared so unsettled? He couldn't have known about Clay's meeting with me. I didn't even know Jared then, so what is it?

CHAPTER THREE

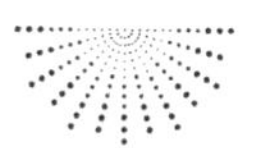

From his room, above the Silver Lady Saloon, Clay Stockton watched Jared and Angelica walk—no run—back toward Jared's house. He laughed. They ran like Clay would shoot them…which he might have, if it wouldn't have been so obvious who had done it.

He dropped the curtain back in place, sending the room into shadow with only a low oil lamp providing light.

"Clay, honey, come back ta bed."

He owned the Silver Lady Saloon and his rooms were lavishly decorated. His bed was heavy oak as were the other pieces of furniture in the room. Now, he looked at the blonde in his bed and couldn't help but compare her to Angelica, whose dark hair and eyes left him wanting to know more, wanting to have her for his own. He'd known, as soon as he saw her in Carson City that she was the one for him.

When he found out she was Jared Winslow's mail-order bride, well, nothing would have been sweeter than to see the look on Winslow's face when Clay took his bride as his own. But she'd turned him down flat. She would rather marry someone she didn't know and hadn't met, rather than marry Clay. If he'd had her alone, he would have convinced her he was the man for her, but they hadn't been alone. They hadn't even been inside somewhere. They'd been standing outside the Carson City Hotel. He was leaving from his most recent liaison. She was waiting for the stage to Virginia City.

On impulse he'd boarded the stage, tied his horse behind the coach and spent the entire sixteen miles, more than three hours, trying to change her mind.

He laughed again

The blonde in the bed came up behind him. "What's so funny, Clay, honey? Did I do something?"

"No. It's nothing to do with you, get back in bed."

He'd been a fool. She didn't even know him but she kept her distance like he was a leper. What did she know just by looking at him that made her stay away? Kept her from taking him up on his offer?

Clay walked to the cheval mirror, something he'd bought so he could gaze upon himself. He looked in it, lifted one brow, rolled the end of his mustache between his thumb and forefinger and used his other hand to smooth his hair back from his temple. Nothing he saw explained what Angelica saw that made her turn him away.

He was a find figure of a man.

So why didn't she see that, too?

Angelica and Jared managed to walk like respectable people the remainder of the way home.

When they arrived, he scooped her into his arms.

She wrapped her arms around his neck. "Jared! You don't have to do this."

"I'm carrying my bride over the threshold of our home. Am I doing it wrong?"

She began to laugh.

He laughed, too, and carried her into the house, shutting the door with a kick from his boot. Then he carried her right up the stairs and to their bedroom. He tossed her on to the bed and came down beside her.

Angelica clasped her hands together in front of her. *He's very handsome and I know he can demand his husbandly rights, but I don't believe he's that way. I need to know someone for more than a couple of hours before I let him make love to me.* "Jared, I thought you said we weren't going to make love."

He dragged his fingers lightly up her arm. "No, what I said was that wasn't the reason I was in a hurry to get you home. And that was true. But now that we're home, I find I'd like nothing better than to make love."

Angelica rolled away from him and off the other side of the bed. "Well, I'm not ready to make love. I know I'm a widow and not some girl just out of the schoolroom, but I would like to know my husband for more than just a couple hours before I jump into bed with him."

Jared stood. "Of course, you do. I guess I just thought since we had talked some before the wedding and—"

"And because I took a bath downstairs before we were married that bit of talking was all the getting to know you I needed. Right?"

He ran a hand behind his neck. "Right."

"Well, I admit this situation is as much my fault as yours…maybe all my fault. I should have gotten a room at the hotel, regardless of the cost."

"Angel, it's not your fault. I knew what I was doing and I just got carried away." He started toward the door. "Now, would you like to change clothes and meet me in the kitchen? I'll go put on a pot of coffee."

"I'd like that. I have a couple changes of clothes in my second carpetbag, which I'll wear until I can get into my trunks and iron everything in them."

Jared stopped at the door and turned back. "Angel?"

She looked up, eyes wide. "Yes."

"Just change your clothes. You don't need to let me know all the where's and why's, just do it."

Heat infused her cheeks and she knew she blushed. "Of course. I'll be down in a few minutes." *It will be nice not to have to explain every little thing I do, like I did with Michael. I loved him, but I now realize Michael was a bit controlling.*

Once he left she hurried out of her dress. With the many small buttons up the front, instead of in back, it still took her a bit to get out of the dress. From her second carpetbag, she pulled a simple cotton dress. She left on one petticoat and bloomers and donned a corset before putting on the blue gingham dress and heading downstairs.

In the kitchen she found Jared sitting at the table.

Upon seeing her, he stood.

"Don't stand. I don't expect you to stand each time I enter a room. We're married, and you can stop using company manners just for me. That's not to say I want you running about the house in your drawers, but staying seated is just fine."

He chuckled. "Fine." He pulled out her chair. "I can still pull out your chair, regardless of what you say."

Laughing she sat. "All right."

He smiled and ran his hand behind his neck. "I just put on a fresh pot of coffee. It'll take about fifteen minutes to boil."

"That's all right. Tell me a bit more about yourself, Jared. I know the bit we exchanged in our letters but that wasn't really very much."

Jared looked down. "There's not a whole lot more to say. I was a Pinkerton detective and then I came here."

Angelica narrowed her gaze. "I don't believe that is all. Why did you leave Chicago and the Pinkerton Agency? There's something you're not telling me."

"What makes you think there's more? There's nothing important you need to know."

"Jared, you're not looking me in the eyes when you talk about the Pinkerton Agency. We have to be honest with each other if this marriage is going to work."

"Of course, I know that. Very well." He stood and paced between the table and the back door. "About a year ago, I was framed. Supposedly, I murdered a local prostitute. I had to come here to stay free until my innocence can be proved. If I'd been arrested, my guilt would have been assured and I'd be rotting in prison now. I know, I probably shouldn't have run. It makes me look guilty, but I swear I did not kill that woman." Jared stopped and stared. "Do you believe me, Angel?"

She stared back at him, eyes narrowed and eyebrows furrowed. She stared at the man she'd written one letter to from the Brides for the West agency, accepting his proposal and she had just the one letter from him. Was he the man she met? The one easy to make smile, who winked at her, laughed with her, was a gentleman while she bathed. Or was he the cold-blooded murderer of a prostitute?

She stood, walked to him, took one of his hands in both of hers. "I believe you, Jared. I don't believe the man I married is capable of murdering a woman or anyone else. The man I married loves the law, that's why even when he's supposed to be laying low, hiding from the law, he can't. He still has to be the law where there is none. I'm aware of the kind of place Virginia City is. I read about it on the way here. If not for you and your deputies, the town would be lawless and the criminals would be running things. With you here, there's a chance for every good man and woman to make a life here."

Jared reached up and wiped a tear from her cheek. "You really are my angel. No one else would believe me in such a short amount of time." He cupped her face. "Thank you." He pulled his hand from hers and then wrapped his arms around her.

She didn't stop him. Not when he pulled her close or when he lowered his head and took her lips with his. Nope, Angelica, kissed him back for all she was worth. When he would have pulled back, she took his face between her palms and kept him close.

She was the one who pressed her tongue against his and begged him for entrance. Michael had taught her to kiss this way and she liked it.

So, apparently, did Jared, for he responded by holding her tighter. Moving his lips from hers to her neck and he kissed up and down its length before returning to her lips.

The kiss went on so long the coffee started boiling over and spattering on the hot stove.

"Jared."

"Hmm?" He kept kissing her.

"The coffee."

He lifted his head. "I should let us do what we came down here to do."

She lifted her brows and nodded.

He let go of her and walked to the stove, grabbed a pot holder and brought the coffeepot to the table. Then he got two cups from the cupboard to the left of the sink.

Angelica used the potholder to pick up the coffeepot, filling both of their cups with the hot, black brew. Then she returned the pot to the stove before sitting again.

"So, Angel, tell me about Michael." He reached across the table and took her hand in his.

The care with which he asked showed he really wanted to know.

"He was the love of my life. We were married for five years. He was a doctor, and a good one. He had a nice practice. We had a nice home and could have had nice children." She closed her eyes and swallowed hard. Her fingernails dug into her palm before she yanked her hand off the table into her lap. "I'm sorry. I always get angry when I think about all we could have had if he had just stayed home. But Michael had to go to war and do his part. He was the first in his family to attend college and the first to be a doctor. He wanted all of America to know the Irish loved their adopted country."

Jared clasped the hand that remained. "Shhh. Take it easy. Breathe. That's right. Breathe." He breathed with her. "Deep breaths. Slowly."

Finally, she began to calm. "I'm sorry. I just get so angry at him. We would have had a family now." She looked away from him and whispered. "I lost our child two days after I got word of his death. The grief of both those losses nearly broke me but I came back, out of that dark place and I don't ever want to return."

"I'm not asking you to. I want you to go forward...with me."

She smiled. "I want to have a life with you, too. I really do but I warn you I might get angry now and again."

"We'll face that issue when we come to it."

Angelica gazed into his eyes. "Tell me about the prostitute in Chicago. What happened?"

Jared shrugged. "Not much to say. She was beaten and then her throat slit. Grisly murder. The person who did it enjoyed the act."

Her eyebrows knitted together and she cocked her head. "Why do you say that?"

"Because there wasn't a place on her torso that wasn't bruised, and her face was battered so badly they identified her by a birthmark on her buttock."

Angelica's fist flew to her mouth to keep from screaming in empathy for the young woman. She swallowed several times and breathed in deeply to get control of herself. "Why do they think you did this heinous crime?"

"A tie like mine was found at the scene."

She shook her head. "Just finding a tie makes no sense. Any man could've worn a tie like that, couldn't they?"

He closed his eyes. "They could have, but the way it was tied around her mouth…the knot was not average. It was in the same unique knot I use."

"I still don't see how the police could think it was you."

Eyes still closed, he clenched his jaw. "I'd been known to visit her on occasion. Not often, mind you, but…"

"Oh." *I wonder if Michael ever visited a prostitute before we married. Would I have looked askance at him if he did? Would I have married him if I'd known? Would I have married Jared if we'd had this conversation before we married? I just don't know.* She didn't say anything for the longest time until finally breaking the silence, "I suppose a man has needs."

"That's no excuse. She was a nice young woman by the name of Renee. She said she was forced into the business to support herself and her son."

"Did she really have a son?"

He shook his head.

His grip on her hand staying constant…tight but not painful.

"I don't know. I never saw a child."

Angelica raised her other hand from her lap and placed it over his. "I refuse to believe you murdered anyone, and nothing you've told me so far has changed my mind. Is there more I should know?"

Jared thought for a moment and then shook his head. "That's all they had against me, that I'm aware of. It's all circumstantial, but it's enough to have me spending my life in prison. That's why I left. My partner is working to clear me and will inform me when that has happened. I'll be able to go back to Chicago."

She lowered her gaze to their hands on the table. "Is that what you want? To go back to Chicago? Do you want to be a Pinkerton agent again"

He tilted his head. "I don't know. Virginia City has grown on me and in the last year, I've made some good friends and found a beautiful wife. Besides, I don't like what I did as a Pinkerton. We were paid to do some terrible things and I want to be part of the law, the answer, not part of the problem. But I don't honestly know at this point what I'll decide to do."

She ducked her head, but the compliment pleased her. "What now?"

"Now, if we aren't spending the afternoon making love…" He looked at her with a hopeful look and puppy dog eyes.

Unable to help herself, she chuckled. "And we're not."

Jared heaved a big sigh. "Then I must go back to

work, but if you like you can come with me on my rounds."

"That would be wonderful. I have to meet the merchants, find out which ones you have accounts with and which ones I will need cash at. I need to know which stores you frequent and which you refuse to and why."

He stood. "Let's go then. We can kill two birds with one stone."

Angelica stood, the coffee, cups still full, forgotten on the table.

As they walked through the house to the front door, she couldn't help but wonder if her trust was misplaced. What did she really know of the man she'd married? Was he a murderer?

CHAPTER FOUR

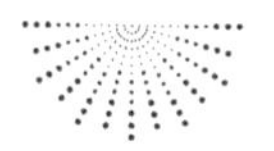

Once they were outside he took her arm again. "I think this activity is a good idea. I get to show off my lovely wife."

Angelica's cheeks heated. "That's very kind of you. I'm glad you think me attractive."

Jared laughed. "Now you're just fishing for a compliment."

She laughed, as well. "Maybe I like them."

He patted her hand. "I'll make sure to tell you often enough you won't feel deprived."

They walked down the left side of the street and into the mercantile.

A black-haired man, several inches shorter than Jared and wearing a dirty white apron greeted them. "Jared. Good to see you. I heard you got married this morning." He turned to her. "You must be Angelica.

That's all the information we could get out of the preacher. I'm Roscoe Brown and I own this shop."

She laughed and put out her hand. *Who does he mean by we?* "Yes, I'm Angelica. There's not a lot to know about me. I'm a widow and a mail-order bride. That sums it up."

"No children?"

She put a hand over her stomach remembering the baby she lost. "No, no children." She looked up at Jared.

Jared quickly said, "We've got a few more shops to stop by. Good to see you Roscoe."

"You, too, Jared." Roscoe took Angelica's hand and kissed the top. "Mrs. Winslow."

"Angelica, please." She pulled her hand back, unused to having her hand kissed by a friend much less a stranger.

"Angelica it is. See you back here soon."

She nodded as Jared pulled her out the door and stopped at the corner of the building.

"I'm sorry he asked about children. I know it must still be painful to talk about."

She looked down at her clasped hands, forced them apart and then looked up at Jared. "Yes, it is. Do you have an account at the mercantile? And what about the butcher we are about to visit?" She needed to change the subject, thinking about children hurt too much.

"I do have an account at both places. I'll only take you introduce you to the merchants with our accounts.

The others we'll just pass by unless I see something that needs taken care of."

She nodded. "Good. I'm ready now."

They walked next door to the butcher and introduced her to him. He was a blond man with hands and arms that were large from working with heavy meat and wielding his cleaver all day.

"Oscar Mahr, this is my wife, Angelica. I'm sure you'll become great friends since she informs me she knows how to cook." He added under his breath. "And bake."

She put her hand on Jared's arm. "Since we don't have anything to prepare at home, may I buy some pork chops and a small roast for tomorrow?"

"Of course. Would you rather cook? It is your wedding day after all."

"I like to cook and to bake. I doubt we'll support the bakery very much." She chuckled. "Unless, of course, I have been occupied with other things." She turned her attention to the butcher. "Mr. Mahr…er…Oscar, I'd like six nice pork chops, please, and that small beef roast." She pointed toward the meat in the glass case. "Eating out is a treat for sure, but I'll save it until later,

Oscar wrapped up the chops and the roast and gave them to Jared. "Very good, Angelica. You have an eye for my best. My guess is that one," He jutted his chin toward Jared. "Will be gaining some weight."

Continuing on, they completed his rounds. She

learned where he shopped, where he had accounts and where he paid cash.

The only establishment they hadn't gone in was The Red Garter Saloon. "If you need something for a recipe or we run out of the whiskey for medicinal purposes, if I can't get it for you, have Robert MacGregor do it."

Not that she wanted to go into the Red Garter, but now that he inferred she couldn't, she really wanted to. The only place she'd seen Robert MacGregor was at the saloon, so it made sense that she would enter to find him. But she didn't mention that bit of information to Jared.

By the time they returned to the house it was almost five o'clock.

After they entered the kitchen, she turned and placed her hands on Jared's arm. "It's late. Do you have to return to your office today?"

He nodded. "I should let Bill Johnson, my first shift deputy, know that I won't be in to stay, but to watch the office while he gets dinner. His wife usually makes him a pail, but I told him I'd bring him food since I thought we'd be eating out."

"Well, you can still bring him dinner. I got six pork chops remember." She gestured to the package he carried. "I was about to wrap up the second three for another meal, but I'll just fry them all and Bill will have a nice pork chop dinner, if that's all right with you."

"That would be great. You'll have to come with me

when I take him his meal. You'll like him. He's a great deputy and a nice man to boot."

"I'd like that. Do you want to eat before we take his or after?"

"Before." He lifted an eyebrow. I want to know what kind of meal I'm taking my friend."

She frowned in mock anger, then laughed. "I assure you, I'm a good cook, but I'll let you be the judge. I'll put Bill's in the warming oven until we're ready to take it to him. Do you, by chance, have any jars of canned vegetables?"

"As a matter of fact…hey, wait a minute, why would you think I'd have jars of vegetables?"

Angelica grinned. "Because you're a handsome, single man and the wives around here, the few there are, want to make sure you are well taken care of so you will think of them before you arrest their husbands."

Jared smiled and shook his head. "You're right, I do have lots of jars of fruit and vegetables. Let's look in the pantry to see what we have."

He opened the door and lit the oil lamp on the counter just inside.

Below the counter, sat bins for flour, sugar and corn-meal. Above were shelves, loaded with jars of food.

"Don't you ever eat at home? You have more vegetables, fruit, jams and jellies than I think the mercantile had."

Jared ran a hand behind his neck. "I didn't know how to say *no* to anyone."

"Well, I'm glad. These will be wonderful for our meals and for pies and cobblers, too."

He perked up, eyes twinkling. "Really? Pies and cobblers?" He rubbed his stomach in circles. "Mmmm. I can't wait."

She nodded. "Yes, pies, cobblers, cakes, cookies, bread and muffins. You name it and I can bake it or cook it and if I don't know how, I'll figure it out. I'm good at asking questions of other wives, when I meet them, and usually between us, we all find our answers."

"Then I'll leave it to you. Do you need my help making dinner?"

"Not unless you want to peel potatoes." At the pained look that crossed his face, she rolled her eyes. "Go into the living room and read the paper or something."

"Actually, I thought I might stay in here and talk while you cook."

She lifted and eyebrow. "You can try but I won't guarantee I'll answer. When I get to cooking and baking, I don't respond to much else." Angelica stopped for a moment. "Actually, I didn't see any potatoes in the pantry. Do you have a root cellar?"

"I do. It would be ridiculous to build a house like this and not put in a root cellar."

"True. Please bring up six good sized potatoes, a bunch of carrots, if you have them, would be welcome as well."

"I'll be right back."

She watched him leave through the back door. Now what would she have him do next to keep him busy? *It's so nice to be in a house with another person, but I don't want to talk about my life anymore.*

Digging through all the drawers she finally found the vegetable peeler.

Jared appeared at the back door carrying a burlap bag. "I brought you potatoes, carrots and onions. They usually go together, right?"

"That's great. I'll need the onions for tomorrow's roast. And look what I found." She grinned and held up the peeler. "Just in time for you to peel the potatoes for tonight's dinner."

After Angelica filled a pie tin with two pork chops, mashed potatoes, gravy and glazed carrots, she and Jared walked Bill's meal over to him. She'd made a cobbler with some of the canned peaches and had that in a separate pie tin. She carried the cobbler and Jared the dinner.

The marshal's office and jail was on Main Street near the blacksmith, on the opposite end of town from where their house was located. Luckily, it was a lovely evening for a stroll as it had cooled from the heat of the day. The sky was filled with millions of tiny stars, sparkling like diamonds. The light summer breeze carried a scent. She stopped and sniffed. "Lilacs. My second favorite scent. I'd love to have some bushes of them in our yard."

"I'll see what I can do."

At the office, Jared opened the door for her. Inside, sitting behind the only desk in the room was a thin man with a scraggly beard and graying brown hair.

He looked up from the desk and stood when he saw her.

"Mrs. Winslow, please have a seat."

A single wooden chair with a latticed back was in front of the desk. The wall behind the chair was filled with wanted posters. In the opposite corner from the desk was a pot-bellied stove.

"Thank you, Bill. Please call me Angelica. I have a feeling we'll spend more time together and get to know each other well. Jared says you're married. Tell me about your family." She set her plate on the desk and then sat.

Jared placed his pie tin on the desk, too. Then he stood next to Angelica, with a hand on her shoulder.

Bill sat again. "Sure. I got my Rosie and we got five kids. John is twelve, Matt is ten, the twins, Scott and Ralph, are six and my baby girl, Martha, is one. I don't know how Rosie does it but she keeps all those kids toeing the line. They're good kids, and I love'em all. I think Martha will be the queen bee of the house, though. She already has the boys dancin' to her tune." He laughed.

Angelica smiled. Her own child would have been

nearly a year old now if…*No! I won't think about my baby and what could have been. I will think of now. Jared and I will have children of our own.*

Not if you don't make love you won't.

Stop it! I just got married today. Let me be. Let me know him more.

You know him enough to know he will be the father of your children.

Tonight is soon enough to make love.

With that issue resolved in her mind, she gazed at Bill as he talked about his children. She might as well start making friends. "Bill, you and Rosie must come for dinner one day soon." She swung her gaze to Jared. "Is there a way both of you can be off on the same night?"

"Sure, I'll talk to Walter Barber and see if he'll change shifts with Bill that night, but I don't see a problem. He's my fourth deputy. My third deputy is Seth Adams. He works the late night shift and he'll be jealous that Bill is coming to dinner. We'll have to ask them both to dinner, with their families. I actually have many more deputies, about twenty-five altogether and I still need more, but these men are closest to me.

"The town is growing by leaps and bounds. Houses are being built at a furious pace up the hillsides. I just don't have enough men right now."

She smiled. "I'd love to have all your men and their families over eventually. The more people I meet the better."

Jared stared at her for a moment. "That's a good attitude to have. I'd hoped you wouldn't be a shrinking violet."

She glanced at him and then moved her gaze to her skirt. Her face heated to little points in her cheeks. "I'm afraid I'm the opposite. I'm very outgoing and I love meeting new people…for the most part…I could have done without meeting Clay Stockton."

He frowned. "That's a good attitude as far as Stockton is concerned."

"Oh, well yes, I suppose it is. Now back to Bill who we have so rudely ignored. Would you like to come to dinner, you and the whole family?"

Bill didn't even stop to think for a moment. "Yes, ma'am, Angelica. We'd like that very much." His mouth turned down a little at the corners. "Any time Rosie doesn't have to cook is a happy time for all of us. My Rosie is a great mother and wife, but a terrible cook."

"Oh dear, but I'm glad you'll all come." She looked over at Jared. "I don't remember, do we have table and chairs to accommodate this many people?"

"Of course. In the dining room."

She shook her head. "I'm afraid I didn't pay attention to the size of the table and number of chairs when we looked in."

"It will accommodate sixteen people."

Angelica looked up at Jared who stood to the side and slightly behind her. "Wonderful. Let's do this in one week. That will give me time to test some recipes on Jared and for you to get schedules switched."

Her husband held out his hand. "We should get home and get those dishes done. I'd like to get to bed early." He winked.

Her eyes widened and then closed for a moment as she realized he was flirting. "We do have to do them tonight. I hate waking up to a messy kitchen." She turned to Bill. "And I want you to eat your dinner while it is still sort of warm."

Bill stood. "Thank you for the wonderful meal. I look forward to eating it."

Jared grasped her hand, and they left the office.

"You are a very naughty man."

He stopped walking and turned to her, cocking his head and one eyebrow. "How am I naughty?"

"Winking at me in front of Bill." She chuckled. "Naughty, naughty."

Jared patted her hand on his arm and started walking again. "I guess there's no getting anything over on you."

"You're a strange man, Jared Winslow. A very strange man."

He laughed. "No, my dear, I'm just a man, no more and no less."

She felt giddy. That was the only way to describe it. Her husband liked to tease her. Michael never had. He was always so serious. Even when they made love, there was never any laughter, or playfulness involved. Angelica always felt like he had something he would rather do.

She looked at her new husband and just shook her head.

He watched her and laughed harder.

What had she said that was so funny? She began to chuckle, his laughter infectious.

If only her marriage could always be this happy but it can't. It won't. She'd loved Michael with all her heart and yet he'd eventually pushed her away, preferring his books to her company.

How long before Jared does the same thing?

CHAPTER FIVE

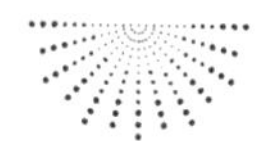

Her first day of marriage had gone well. She and Jared talked and knew a little more about each other, which was good. Now, the day was over, and bedtime was here. Even though she was not a virgin and knew exactly what to expect, she was nervous. What if Jared didn't like her body? She wasn't young and willowy, she was old and she'd never been willowy in her life.

Angelica quickly changed into her nightgown while Jared locked the house. He told her he would check the windows and doors, making sure they were all secure. Virginia City was a rough-and-tumble town where you never knew who might break into your house to steal something worth gambling away. The fact that he was the marshal made no difference to a desperate man.

When he finally came in he stared at her and cocked

up a brow. "You won't need the nightgown, not tonight or ever."

She quickly finished hanging her dress and lifted her chin. "I like having a layer of cloth between us."

"I don't. I want to feel your body. Feel your skin next to mine. Surely Michael didn't want you in a nightgown. Did he?"

She shook her head and sat on the bed, her back to him. *On their wedding night Michael had asked but never demanded that she remove her gown. She'd been so scared because she had no idea what to expect. Now, was different. She was scared for the opposite reasons. She did know what to expect.* "But he'd been with me through all the changes in my body. You haven't. I'm not a young woman with a young body. My breasts are not perky. Actually, they've never been perky. Oh, Jared, what if you hate my body?"

He came around the bed and sat on the side of it next to her.

His shirt was unbuttoned and she couldn't help but admire his chest. His stomach was flat and muscular and he had just a sprinkling of dark hair covering the top. Michael was also dark haired but he'd had much more hair on his chest than Jared.

Would she always be making these comparisons between her two husbands?

Angelica couldn't look at him.

Jared gently took the knuckle of his forefinger and his thumb and turned her head toward him. "Is that what bothers you? Angel, I'm not a young man with a young man's body. Does that repulse you?"

"No. Of course, not."

"Then why would you think your body would bother me? You're beautiful. All of you. What'll it take for me to prove that to you?"

"I don't know."

"Come, take off your gown and let me make love to you. All of you." He rose and held out his hand.

Angelica took a deep breath and stood by the side of the bed, in front of him. She whipped the nightgown over her head and dropped it on the floor beside the bed. Then she waited in front of him with her eyes closed. A flush warmed her skin and she realized she was excited as well as nervous and afraid.

After a minute or two, he said, "Angel, open your eyes."

She opened them and then widened them as she saw he was nude. "Oh," she gasped. "Oh, my."

His mouth turned up on one side. "Do you see something you dislike? Do I repulse you?"

"No, yo…you're glorious."

"As are you."

"But I—"

Whatever she'd been about to say was lost in the feel of his lips on hers.

He wrapped her in his arms and pulled her close. "You will always be beautiful to me. You're my Angel, remember?"

"I know, but—" His strong arms held her close and she registered the feeling building in her. Safe. She was safe in his arms. Angelica was no longer alone, would no longer have to endure long, lonely nights.

He covered her lips with two fingers. "Shh. I won't hear any more buts from you." He removed his fingers and replaced them with his lips. He lifted her arms and she wrapped them around his neck. Keeping his lips on hers, Jared laid her onto the bed and came down after her.

He pulled back but kept her in his arms. "I'm making love to you now, Angel."

"I'm ready for you to."

He took her lips again and then made love to her.

Angelica had never had anyone make love to her like Jared did. Her pulse raced at the memory. Now, tucked into his side, with his arms still around her, she felt loved. They barely knew each other, but she couldn't help the feelings that threatened to overwhelm her. Did Jared have these feelings, too?

Was she being unfaithful to Michael?

Angelica was cutting out biscuits to bake as part of a special breakfast. She thought on their six week anniversary she would treat Jared to a full breakfast with eggs, bacon, sausage, biscuits and some of the chokecherry jam she found in the pantry. These women liked Jared a lot as she found many, many jars of jams, jellies and canned fruits and vegetables.. Were they thinking he would marry them or were they bribing him to marry their daughters? The reasons didn't matter. What did matter is she and Jared would be enjoying the fruits of their labor for some time to come.

Bam! Bam! Bam!

The pounding on the back door startled her. "Just a minute." She wiped her hands on a kitchen towel while she unlocked and opened the door.

Bill practically bowled her over.

"Sorry, Angelica. Where is Jared?"

"He's not come down yet. Why don't you have a—"

"I'm here." Jared walked in, buttoning his cuffs. "What's wrong, Bill?"

"There's been a murder, Jared. That new whore at The Red Garter. I think Vanessa is her name, anyway she was found—" he stopped abruptly. "Angelica you might not want to stay for the details."

"I'm fine. Tell Jared what he needs to know."

Jared put his arm around her shoulders.

Bill took a deep breath. "She was found with her throat slashed. It's a mess in there, Jared. Don't wear your good boots."

"Oh, my God." Gasping Angelica put a hand to her mouth to keep from screaming. How could anyone do that to someone else?

Jared turned her and held her by both shoulders. "I have to go now. I want you to calm down. Investigating crime is what I do, remember? I'm the marshal here. I'm the law and I have to find out who did this, and quickly."

She nodded. "I know. I understand. Go. I'll be fine. I have shopping to do and I'll find Robert. He can go with me. He said if I needed him, he was here for me."

"That's a good idea. I don't like the idea of you being by yourself. Come with me. I'll walk you there since that's where I'm going anyway."

He waited while Angelica covered the biscuits with a couple of tea towels. *I'll bake these when I get back.*

She pinned her watch on the left side of her chest, grabbed her shawl and her reticule and then Jared took her hand and they headed for The Red Garter. Angelica didn't know where else to find Robert, so it made sense to start there. When they arrived, she took a deep breath and started in.

Jared stopped her. "You can't go in there. I'll send Robert out when I see him. You wait right here."

Bill was waiting for them outside the saloon.

Jared released her hand. "Good. Bill, I want you to wait here with Angelica. If I see Robert I'll send him out."

She waited with Bill. Angelica paced back and forth on the boardwalk. She would stop and look over the swinging doors and then pace again.

"Angelica?"

She turned toward the deep bass voice. "Oh, Robert.

I've been trying to get my courage up to go into the Red Garter to find you."

He chuckled. "I admit I spend a lot of time here but I don't live here."

"I came to see if you would accompany me on my shopping errands today...that is if you don't have something else you must do." She turned to Bill. "Thanks for waiting with me. You can go find Jared now."

Bill tipped his hat to her then to Robert. "Got to go."

Robert smiled and answered her question. "Don't worry about it. I make me own hours."

"It's nice your employer allows that."

He chuckled. "I am me employer. I own the Molly Girl mine."

Her face heated. "Oh, you must think me a dolt."

Robert took her hand and tucked it into the crook of his elbow. "Of course, not. Now let's go get yer errands done. By the way, why would you need me ta come with you ta do your errands today?"

"Jared didn't want me to be alone. A prostitute named Vanessa was murdered last night. She—"

Robert stopped walking. "Vanessa?"

"That's right. Did you know her?"

"I did. She was a good woman. She was new here. Had only been here a couple of months. I know she was a prostitute, but I liked her, I was even thinking about asking her to marry me."

She put her free hand on his arm. "Oh, Robert, I'm so sorry."

Robert looked down at her. “Do you suppose we could do your errands on another day?”

“Of course. Would you mind walking me home?”

“Not at all, then I’ll find Jared. I must tell him what I know.” He turned them back toward her home.

“He’s at The Red Garter. What do you know that you think Jared might need?”

The sound of their boots on the boardwalk was almost too loud for them to be heard as they talked. “Vanessa confided that she was afraid of one of her clients.”

Angelica gazed up at Robert. “Did she say which one?”

He shook his head. “She wouldn’t give me his name. She knew I’d kill him. Now, I wish I’d pushed her to tell me. If I’d just asked her to marry me. If she’d said yes, I’d have taken her out of there and put her up in the hotel until we got married. If I’d have asked her, she’d be alive today.”

She stopped and turned toward him. “Robert, you can’t think like that. You don’t know that for sure. She might have refused, or she might have decided to work until you got married. You’ll never know what she would have done.”

As they got closer to her house, she saw someone run away and suddenly stopped walking. Did you see that?”

He nodded and stood straighter. “I’ll enter the house first and make sure it’s safe.”

She nodded and tightened her hold on his arm. "Thank you, I'd appreciate that."

Arriving at the house they stopped at the bottom of the steps up to the porch.

Robert released her and drew his pistol. "Wait here." With his gun out he entered the house.

A few minutes later he came out. "Everything looks fine and there is no one inside. I want you to go in, lock the doors. I'll come with ye and do the windows."

Her shoulders relaxed but her stomach still turned over and made her nauseous. "I don't know how to thank you."

"No thanks are necessary. You're Jared's wife and now you're my friend, just like he is. Besides…I like you."

She had the sudden desire to hug him, so she did. "I like you, too."

Robert walked her through the house to the kitchen and watched her lock the back door.

Then she waited in the kitchen until he returned from locking the windows. She showed him out the front and knew he waited for her to lock the door because she heard his boot falls across the porch as he left.

Angelica leaned her back against the door and then slid down until she was sitting on the floor. *Murder! I've only been here six weeks and there's a woman murdered. Is there a connection or is this strictly a coincidence?*

Angelica knew she couldn't stay on the floor all day, no matter how much she wanted to just sit there and cry, but she wasn't really a crier. Besides, she had things to do—chores to finish.

She walked to the kitchen, lit the oven again, then uncovered the biscuits and baked them. While they baked she began her chores. First she rolled two dish towels and set them about eight inches apart.

Then she went to the bedroom and made the bed. By the time she was finished with the bedroom, the biscuits were done. They were golden on top and she pulled them from the oven and set the pan on the rolled towels which formed a makeshift rack for the pan of bread.

Dusting the house was next. When she was done dusting she swept the floors, then oiled all the wood. These were things she had on her list to do regularly.

Checking her pin watch, she had about half an hour before Jared would be home for lunch…if he came home today. Nonetheless she prepared the planned anniversary breakfast for him since she didn't get to the mercantile. When the bacon was done and still no Jared, she paced between the stove and the back door. Braiding her hair always soothed her with its repetitive motion. She took her hair down and combed through it with her fingers.

When she was half way across the kitchen on a trip back from the door, it suddenly opened and Jared stood there. Though this wasn't the first day she worried about him coming home, this was different. He looked exhausted. She wasn't sure how to soothe him but she knew she needed to hold him right now. Angelica walked to him and put her arms around him.

His arms came around her and tightened. Jared buried his face in the hair at her neck.

"Thank you for being here." He said into her hair.

"Of course, I'm here." She had many things she wanted to ask but felt he needed to hold her tightly right now.

Finally, he pulled back and kissed her forehead. "As many times as I've seen things like this, I'll never get used to it. I can't imagine how no one heard anything. That poor girl."

"Come. Sit and I'll get you a cup of coffee. I'm afraid all we have in the house for food is bacon and eggs. I made biscuits. I know you're probably not hungry, but you need to eat. Jared, are you listening?"

He sat with his head bowed and his hands behind his neck while his elbows were on the table. She served him the coffee. "Maybe just a couple of biscuits with bacon on them. How would that be?"

Jared didn't say anything but nodded.

Angelica prepared two biscuit sandwiches and set the plate in front of him. "Jared. Are you all right?"

He looked up toward her. "I'm sorry. Thank you for the food. I know I need to eat. When I leave again, I want you to lock the door behind me and make sure all the doors are locked and the windows as well."

"I will don't worry. Robert made me do the same thing." *Should I tell him about the man running from the house? I think it better to wait.* "Eat. I'll get you a glass of milk to go with the sandwiches. You need all the nourishment you can get right now. Do you want me to fix you some eggs?"

Jared shook his head. "No. I don't think I could keep them down."

She brought the milk to the table and set it in front of him. Then she sat on his right. "I'm sorry you have to go through this. Did Robert find you?"

Jared shook his head.

"He knew Vanessa. He was even thinking of marrying her. If you get a suspect, you should keep that information close to the vest, for Robert's sake." Sensing Jared needed her touch and she placed a hand on his arm. "I don't really know Robert at all but the man I've met is a good man. I think he must be a good friend to you or you wouldn't have told me to go to him. But I fear if he has any idea of who did this to the poor woman, that man will be dead. You can't let that happen."

He patted her hand as it rested on his arm. "I know and you're right, he is my good friend. He's about the only man here who knows I'm a former Pinkerton agent."

She lowered her chin and narrowed her eyes. "Are

you sure? I get the feeling Clay has a grudge against you."

"Clay Stockton has a grudge against anyone who won't let him do whatever he pleases. He was raised in a wealthy, but cold, family. He never learned to share or to be kind." He pointed at her. "Be careful of Clay Stockton. You turned him down, that's put you on the same list I'm on."

"You seem to know a lot about his background. Why is that?"

"He's originally from Chicago. His family still lives there and…" He paused. "He was a Pinkerton agent until I had him arrested for blackmailing one of our clients. He was also almost my brother-in-law. I was engaged to his sister."

"What?" Her eyebrows practically flew, she lifted them so fast she shook her head. She was quiet for a moment. "Was he convicted of the blackmail? If not, why doesn't Clay still live in Chicago? Virginia City is a strange place to go unless you're running either from something or someone. What is Clay running from? When did he move to Virginia City?"

Jared stood abruptly and began to pace. "After he was thrown out of the Pinkerton's, I was investigating a murder in Chicago. A prostitute, just like here. He was my chief suspect, but I couldn't prove it." He slammed his fist into his other palm. "If I'd proved it then, this murder probably wouldn't have happened. Instead he had evidence planted framing me for the murder. That's the one I'm accused of doing."

She stood leaning against the counter by the sink, her arms crossed over her chest. "You can't know that."

"Oh, but I can." He spat the words at her. "This murder is almost identical to the one in Chicago except that girl..."

"What?"

"She didn't look like you."

"So?"

"Vanessa looked like you."

CHAPTER SIX

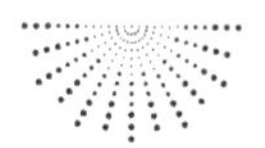

Angelica's hand flew to her neck. She tried to swallow but her throat was suddenly dry. "Like me?"

He closed his eyes and ran his hands through his hair. "Yeah, like you. I wouldn't have thought anything about it if you hadn't told me you turned Stockton down when he asked you to marry him."

She snorted. "He didn't so much ask as order. After I refused, I made sure I was never alone with him. And he still badgered me to marry him for the entire sixteen miles from Carson City, despite the other people in the coach."

"Either way, you turned him, down whether related to his question or his order. Then, as if to rub salt in the wound, you married me. That event could have sent him over the edge. Somehow I don't think it would have taken much."

Clay is much more dangerous than I thought. She stood and walked over to him. "But he knew I was to marry you. As a matter of fact, he didn't seem much interested in me until he found out you were my intended groom. And then I couldn't get rid of him."

He lifted a brow and then furrowed them, his eyes narrow. "Really? That's very interesting. It would seem Stockton moved to Virginia City because of me. I hoped it was coincidence. He and I showed up here at about the same time. I should have known better. When he found out I liked him for the prostitute's murder in Chicago, he had one of his buddies in the Pinkerton's claim to have found new evidence. Evidence that implicated me." He stopped and pulled on the ends of his mustache, rolling them just a bit.

Angelica raised a hand and stopped him from reaching for his mustache again. "Clay rolles his mustache all the time. Please don't you start doing it, too."

He took her hand, brought it to his lips and kissed the palm. "I'll try not to acquire that habit."

She lifted her brow. "I'd rather see you shave it off than start acquiring his habits."

He widened his eyes. "I'll remember." He kissed her palm again. "Trust me."

"I do trust you, and I don't believe that you're a murderer, either. But I think, from what you've said, that Clay is, and if he could plant doubt into the Pinkertons about you, what will he do here?"

"I think he wanted it to be exactly like the Chicago murder and then he could go to the judge and say that I'd done it. The girl in Chicago was blonde and blue eyed, but Vanessa could have been your sister. In this case, I believe he was punishing her for you choosing me over him. And that will be his undoing. He had to have done damage to his hands, so he'll probably be wearing gloves until his hands heal."

"It's September 30th. No one is wearing gloves yet. The weather has been too warm."

"Exactly. He'll stand out. At the very least he'll have to have some explanation when I ask why he's wearing gloves." He grabbed her around the waist and pulled her to him. "Thank you. It's nice to talk to someone." He kissed her.

"What if..."

He pulled back and looked down at her. "What if...what?"

"What if Clay's not wearing gloves?"

Jared released her and turned away and gazed out the window. "That will mean someone else did it, but that would also mean someone else did the Chicago killing and I was wrong."

I know he could be wrong, but something about Clay warned me to keep him at arm's length. He's evil. I can feel it in my bones. "Someone who wants you in jail... out of the way for some reason. Who else is here from Chicago? Who else might know about that murder and be here in Virginia City? Or it could mean that Clay wore gloves when he beat her."

"I don't know. Let's face that problem when we need to…*if* we need to. I don't want to ask for more trouble."

She swallowed and nodded. "You're right."

He hugged her. "Angel, thank you. You don't have any idea how much it means to me to talk to you, to work things out with another person. I don't want to always bring home my work, but that is the nature of the job. Having you here makes all the difference in the world to me."

"Jared." She reached up and cupped his jaw. "You're my husband and I take my vows very seriously. Whatever affects you affects me. I will always be here for you."

He turned his head and kissed the palm of her hand. "Thank you. I take them seriously, too. I will protect you to the best of my ability."

She looked up. "I know you will." *Unless Clay makes it impossible. Why does he want Jared either dead or out of the way? What does Clay want?*

Jared returned to the office after breakfast with Angelica, his angel. He smiled. She really was his angel, whether she realized it or not. He needed someone in his corner for a change, and she was definitely in his.

He walked in and found Bill speaking to a man in a suit with his back to Jared.

Bill looked up. "Ah, here he is now. Jared, this gentleman is here to see you."

The man, with light brown hair, turned.

Jared's mouth fell open and then he grinned as he looked into the sparkling blue eyes of his partner and best friend. "Ken." He held his hand out and walked forward to greet his friend. "What are you doing here? Did you just get into town? What am I saying? Of course, you did." He turned to his deputy. "Bill, this is Ken Barker, my former partner. Ken, Bill here is my chief deputy marshal. I'm taking Ken on my rounds and then home to meet Angelica. Will you handle things until then?"

"Sure. Go ahead. Nothing to do on the current case until Doc gets done with the body."

Jared frowned. "I know." Smiling at Ken, he clapped him around the shoulders. "Come with me on my rounds and then come meet my wife, Angel."

Ken reared back, his blue eyes flashing. "Wife? You? When?"

Jared laughed as he and Ken walked out of the office.

"I broke down and got a mail-order bride, but she's not what you think. She's amazing."

Seeing his friend's frown, Jared laughed again. "Wait. Just wait."

After checking with the downtown businesses they walked to the house. When they reached there, Jared took the key from his vest and opened the front door.

He called out, "Angel. I'm home."

She walked out of the kitchen, wiping her hands on a dish towel. "You're back sooner than I—excuse me. I didn't know we had a guest."

"Angel, this is my partner from my Pinkerton days, Kenneth Barker. Ken, this is Angelica, my wife." Jared looked over at his partner. "Close your mouth, you'll catch flies."

Ken closed his mouth. "Forgive me. I thought you said she was a mail-order bride."

She smiled. "I was." Angelica held out her hand toward Jared. "Now, I'm Jared's wife."

"But…you're not plain…er…I mean—"

Jared laughed. "I got the cream of the crop in my Angel." He wrapped an arm around her waist.

Ken's eyebrows knitted together. "You weren't supposed to be married. I mean I never pictured you being married, though if I'd seen Angelica, I'd have married, too."

Angelica smiled wide. "That's very kind of you."

She stepped away from Jared. "Now, gentlemen, may I get you a cup of coffee? A slice of fresh apple pie?"

"Pie!" said Jared. "You bet. Angel is a great baker. Wait until you taste her apple pie. Or peach, cherry, it doesn't matter they're all good."

She laughed. "Please, stop. My head will be so big I won't get through the door. Now come sit, please."

The men followed her to the kitchen and sat at the table. Jared on the end in his regular chair and Ken to his right.

Angelica brought them each a cup of fresh coffee and then a large piece of the apple pie she'd just baked.

"There you go. Now, you men discuss whatever you came home to discuss. I have housework to do."

Jared smiled and watched her leave. As soon as she was gone, so was his smile. "What's the real reason you're here?"

Ken also sobered. "I'm following a lead."

Jared leaned forward. "Does it concern me?"

"No. I proved the evidence against you was planted. We found additional evidence the girl had hidden. The woman was afraid for her life. She'd written a note and put a cufflink in a box under the bed. The note stated Clay Stockton would be her killer. He apparently liked to beat her up before…"

Jared wrapped his hands around his coffee cup. "I have a suspicion Stockton killed the girl here. He was angry Angel turned him down and then married me. On the stagecoach, he badgered her from Carson City all the way here. She steadfastly refused."

Ken frowned. "What does that have to do with your victim?"

"Vanessa, that's the prostitute, could have been Angel's double. I believe Stockton got carried away and killed her…before he slit her throat."

Ken leaned forward and rested his elbows on the table, his hands clasped. "You think that because this woman resembled Angelica, she's in danger?"

"Yes, I do." Jared looked toward the living room, where Angel had gone. "I don't want her to be afraid, but I also don't want her out of the house without myself or Robert nearby."

"Robert?" Ken widened his eyes and then grinned. "You can't mean Robbie MacGregor, that unofficial partner of yours?"

"Yes, Robert came to Virginia City with me and bought a mine. As it turned out, a profitable one. Until you came, he's the only person I've trusted the entire time I've been here."

"Robbie…er…Robert is a decent man."

"He is, and Angel likes him. That's good enough for me. If she's comfortable with him, then I'll let her do as she wants as long as he's with her."

Ken drank some of his coffee and made a face.

"You should drink it when it's hot. She actually makes a good cup of coffee and we'd better at least take a bite of the pie."

Ken forked a bite of pie into his mouth.

Jared watched his eyes light up.

"This is fantastic." He took another bite.

Laughing, Jared began to eat his own pie. Before long, it was gone, and so was every drop of coffee.

He glanced at Ken, who used his finger to get up every crumb of the pie. Jared grinned. "I take it you like my wife's baking."

"I do. I can't imagine how you haven't become as big as a house."

"Just lucky I guess. Angelica has a great figure, too. But she works hard keeping up with the housework."

Ken rubbed his hands together, removing any left-over crust. "So, back to business. What did you find at this new murder that leads to Clay Stockton?"

Jared leaned forward with his forearms on the table. "He wears a distinctive cufflink, and we found one under Vanessa's body. I'm sure he didn't think to move her once he'd killed her. We had to, so we found the cufflink."

Huffing out a chuckle, Ken said, "That's what we found, too. You'd think Stockton would get smarter and at least buy different cufflinks. Can you show me yours?"

Jared went to the bedroom and returned with the item. "You're lucky I haven't put it in the evidence safe yet. This is it. He wears them all the time." He handed the jewelry to Ken.

He turned it over in his hand. "There are initials on here."

"I know. C.S."

Ken handed the jewelry back to Jared. "This could be the mate to the one we found in Chicago. So how do we prove it was Clay Stockton?"

Jared leaned forward. "Did you really find a cufflink?"

Ken nodded. "Yes, we really did and it was engraved, just like that one and just like mine are." Ken lifted his hands revealing his cufflinks that were just like the one Jared had. "The man who creates these always put the initials of the buyer on them."

"There are a lot of men with the initials CS. How do you know it was Clay?"

"He was seen leaving the scene, remember. And the owner never saw you that night. It should have been easy to prove your innocence before you had to flee, but I understand why you did. I would have done the same considering the atmosphere of the agency at that time. Luckily, I talked the judge into not making you appear in person. He did level a hefty fine though, two-hundred dollars. I'm here to collect it, but I'm helping you solve this murder before I go anywhere." He reached into his inside coat pocket and produced an envelope. "Here are the court papers for your records."

Jared took the envelope and examined the papers. "Thanks for coming, Ken. I know the agency could have sent someone else."

He reached for his empty cup and quickly put it back on the table. "I volunteered. I wanted to make sure you're doing well. And it appears you are doing very well."

"Thanks, Ken. I need all the help I can get."

"You're welcome. Now how do we get Clay Stockton?"

CHAPTER SEVEN

The following morning, Angelica prepared breakfast for her, Jared and Ken. She and Jared insisted Ken stay with them. Jared helped him move from the hotel the previous night.

Jared left for the day, with Ken and without kissing her as he usually did, she assumed because of Ken. A few minutes later he returned, found her doing the dishes and put his arms around her from behind.

He nuzzled her neck. "Bet you thought I forgot to kiss you."

She bent her head to give him the access he requested with his kisses. Her heart raced, shivers ran up and down her spine. "The thought had crossed my mind."

He turned her in his arms and kissed her lips. "Never. I will always kiss you goodbye, hello, good morning and good night. You can count on it and if I forget one, you better find out what is wrong, because I won't ever miss them if I can help it."

He moved from her neck to her lips and kissed her deeply, then he broke off the kiss. "I have to go. I left Ken waiting outside." Jared gave her a quick peck.

Her eyebrows furrowed and her eyes widened. "Tell me you didn't really leave him outside, just waiting? Surely you sent him on to the marshal's office."

"Nope, I'd be lying if I did. He's waiting, but he knows what I came in for and he's fine with it."

She sighed. "All right if you say so. I'll see you tonight. I'm finding Robbie and taking him shopping with me. I thought I'd invite him for dinner, too. The three of you can reminisce. Perhaps over a glass of whiskey or brandy. Can Robbie get that for me at the saloon?"

"Yes, and he'll probably be at the saloon, too."

"Good. I don't want to have to track him down."

Jared walked toward the back door. "You shouldn't. As a matter of fact, I'll send him to get you. Now, got to go. See you tonight. We'll go to the hotel for lunch."

"All right, see you then."

As Jared walked out, Angelica wondered if he loved her. She knew he lusted after her, but did he love her? She knew she loved him and she knew he loved to kiss her and have relations, but was that love? She'd fallen for him almost immediately. Was she being untrue to Michael's memory by loving Jared? She thought Michael would be happy for her. He wouldn't have wanted her to stay a widow forever. Would he?

Bam! Bam! Bam!

Angelica answered the door. Robbie greeted her with a kiss on the cheek. "How is my favorite Angel?"

She smiled and shook her head. "I don't know why you and Jared insist on calling me that. I'm definitely no angel."

"Oh, I bet you are, you just don't realize it."

Angelica chuckled and took his arm. "Well, whatever makes you two happy. Today I need to shop for tonight's dinner and I want you to join us. One of your friends is here from Chicago. Ken Barker." She waited a minute to see his reaction to the news.

Robbie smiled.

Angelica smiled. Jared would be surrounded by his friends tonight. "I'm assuming you'll be over then about six o'clock?"

"Aye, that I will."

"Good. I thought I'd make a pot roast, so I need to visit the butcher as well as the mercantile."

"Shall we be off then, lass?"

In her best brogue she said, "Aye, we be off."

After they left the house, she took his arm, which

was actually about her shoulder height because he was so tall. Angelica steered him to the mercantile first.

"Hello Roscoe," she called to the owner who was behind the counter checking out another customer.

"Good morning, Angelica…Robert."

"Good morning, to ye," said Robert.

Angelica picked up the vegetables. Canning was something she enjoyed and she had plenty of beef broth in the pantry.

Next was the butcher.

"Hi Oscar. I'm preparing pot roast for dinner and I need the biggest chuck roast you have."

"Ah, Angelica and my big Scottish friend, Robert. How are you today?"

Angelica smiled. "I'm fine, thanks for asking. How are you and the missus?"

"Right as rain," said Robert.

"We're both good. The baby is supposed to be here any time now and my Gretchen is ready to have that child in her arms not her belly." He laughed.

"Can't say as I blame her," said Angelica. "Now I'd like that big chuck roast." She pointed toward the glass case. "And the smaller one next to it for good measure. I've got three men with good appetites to feed."

If Robbie ate like Jared and Ken, she'd need every ounce of the four pounds of meat she ended up buying.

Robbie carried all the groceries.

As she led around the corner by the newspaper office just four blocks from home, she heard a shot and

Robbie groaned. The groceries hit the ground just before he did.

"Robbie!" She knelt beside him and felt for a pulse. Thank God, she found one.

"Don't worry about him, Angelica. Worry about me."

She looked up into the face of Clay Stockton who held a pistol in hand. "Clay, what have you done? Are you crazy?"

"Not crazy...desperate. Jared has one of my cufflinks and I need it back. I'm going to trade you for that little piece of evidence."

Angelica stayed stock still, not moving from Robbie's side. She looked at Clay's hands. They were battered. Angelica looked up at him. "You murdered Vanessa."

"It was an accident."

She shook her head. "Slitting her throat after beating her up, is not an accident."

Suddenly the newspaper owner came around the corner. "Hey, what's going on here?"

Clay looked behind him at the small, balding man. "Go back in your office, Charlie, and forget what you saw here, or die. Your choice."

Charlie raised his hands and hurried back inside.

Turning back to Angelica, Clay frowned. "Now, as to Vanessa, she provoked me. I knew when I met you the first time that you looked like Vanessa. But she knew you as well and knew she resembled you."

. I need to keep him talking. Hopefully, Charlie ran for Jared. Please let him have gone for Jared. "Why is that a reason to kill her? Did you imagine she was me?"

"Yes. No. I don't know." He regained control of himself. "What I do know is you're coming with me, now."

She looked around, hoping for another person, then put up her hands and backed away slowly. "Clay, you don't want to do this. Jared doesn't love me; he'll never trade you for the evidence."

He waved the gun. "Stop moving."

Pulse racing, her breath came in short pants. She stopped immediately.

"I'm betting you're wrong and you better pray I'm right, because if I'm not I won't have any choice but to kill you and run."

Her heart pounded so hard she thought it would burst from her chest. "Why would you kill me?"

He never lowered the gun. "Because you can testify against me if I'm caught."

She shook her head. "I won't. I promise Clay. I'll never tell anyone."

"I can't take that chance." Clay waved the pistol again. "Start walking."

Angelica realized she couldn't count on anyone but herself. So she did what Clay said for now and hoped Charlie went for Jared.

Two horses were tied behind the buildings.

"I hope you can ride because even if you can't

you're coming with me. The journey will be easier if you know how to ride."

"I do, though I've never used a saddle like that one." She pointed toward the horses and looked around still hoping for help from someone…anyone.

"Doesn't matter. I'll have the reins so you don't run. I don't want to have to shoot you, too. Now, get on that strawberry roan."

She went to the horse and mounted easily.

He mounted the black, holding the reins to her horse. Then he kicked the horse in the side until they were galloping toward the mountains.

She held on to the horn and watched for landmarks she could use when she came back this way. Angelica had no illusions that escaping would be easy, but she *would* escape. She *would* warn Jared, because she had no doubt Clay would kill him rather than stand trial for murder. After all, what was one more murder to him?

After about two hours, Clay veered off the main road to a much less traveled path. The trees were so thick she wasn't sure she could find her way back but she would try. They couldn't be more than fifteen or so miles from town, even though they'd galloped most of the way.

Finally, the trees parted, and a small clearing appeared. In the back of the clearing stood a two-story cabin made of rough hewn logs. A hitching post was out front .

Clay pulled the horses to a stop when they reached it.

He turned in his saddle and barked orders at her. "Get down. Now."

Angelica complied, her legs shaky since she hadn't ridden in some time. He must think she couldn't find her way back or that it was too far to walk because he didn't hold his gun on her.

He might be right about it being too far to walk. But she could walk it but maybe not before he caught up with her. But, if she took one of the horses, she'd make it back easily.

Angelica stood by the horses, waiting for Clay's next order.

"Get in the house and make us some food. The steak, eggs and milk in the icebox are fresh. I brought them up here yesterday."

She nodded and headed inside. The front door opened into the living room. To her left was a hallway. She ran down it. *Maybe there's a back door*. At the end she found the small kitchen, but no back door. Angelica wouldn't let the lack of a back exit defeat her. She went immediately to the drawers looking for a knife or something she could injure Clay with and then she could get away. There was nothing big enough, just a paring knife and a steak knife. The knife in her boot was bigger than either of those and still wasn't big enough to do sufficient damage before he took it away from her. Angelica wasn't willing to try with her knife. She knew he would have to tie her up if he was to go back to town. She would need it to get free if he tied her up and she was fairly sure he would.

Angelica walked to the icebox and found two steaks, eggs and milk. She took out one steak and the eggs. Bread was on a plate on the counter. In the lower cupboard nearest the icebox were pots and pans. She pulled out two cast iron skillets and set them on the stove.

She found long wooden matches in a box on top of the warming oven.

After lighting the stove, she let the skillets heat. *Can I hit him over the head with a skillet?* She looked around for someplace to hide so she could surprise him, but there was none. She'd have to stand to one side of the door and hit him then. Maybe while he was down she could get a bridle on a horse. That's all she needed. Angelica was an excellent horsewoman but Clay didn't need to know that.

She grabbed one of the heavy skillets and stood to the left side of the door. As soon as he passed her she swung the cast iron pan and hit him on the back of the head.

Dropping the skillet, she ran for the front door, threw it open and flew to the barn.

Inside she grabbed a bridle and put it on the roan. Then she led it outside and swung up on its back. She kicked the horse to a gallop and headed out past the house.

When she looked back she still didn't see Clay. *Maybe I killed him. If I did, he deserved it.*

What if Clay catches me before I can get to Jared?

She wouldn't think of that possibility now but would ride as fast as she could. Her hair came loose from the knot at her nape and flew wild behind her. She reached town and rode directly to the doctor's office to check on Robert, hoping Jared would also be there.

When she walked in, windblown and out of breath, she saw Jared sitting in the outer office. Her body sagged in relief.

"Oh, thank God. How is Robert? Will he be all right?" She placed her hands on Jared's chest. "Oh, Jared, Clay shot him and then kidnapped me. He took me to his hunting lodge in the mountains. It's about two hours from town and—"

He wrapped his arms around her. "Shhh. Slow down. First things first. Robert will be all right. The bullet hit him in the middle of his back. It didn't hit any vital organs or his spine. Doc says he'll be laid up for a couple of weeks." He eased back, while still keeping his arms loosely around her. "I told him he'd come and stay with us while he recovers."

"Oh, yes, of course. I'll take care of Robert. It's my fault he got shot." She looked down and bit the inside of her cheek to keep from crying. "If he hadn't been with me…" Despite her efforts, tears ran down her cheeks.

With a knuckle under her chin, he raised her head so she looked at him. "His injury is not your fault, and

Robert would be the first to tell you so. He's a good friend and came to Virginia City to help me get evidence on Clay. He knew the risks." He took her lips with his and gave her a light kiss. "Now, ease your mind. All will be well. I will arrest Clay for kidnapping you. I'm just so glad you found your way home. Bill is out looking for you now. He's the best tracker I have. If anyone can find that cabin...or hunting lodge of Clay's he can. He's the best I've got for this, better than me. That's why I sent him."

"Didn't Charlie Cooper find you? He saw what happened."

"He didn't." Jared frowned. "I'll have to have a talk with Charlie. In the meantime as soon as we hear from the doctor about Robbie. Now that I know where he is, I'll get him."

Her heart was a little lighter just being in Jared's arms. "I hit him with a cast iron skillet. I don't know if I killed him or not. If I did, it was self-defense."

"Don't worry about that. Here's the doctor now."

Doctor Schossow, entered the room from the hallway, wiping his hands on a towel. He was a tall man, at least as tall as Jared with black hair slicked back from a middle part. "Jared, I'm glad you're still here." He turned to her. "Angelica, I'm happy you're here, too. Robert is awake and asking for both of you. Follow me, please."

Jared took her hand and they followed the doctor.

Robert sat up in the clinic's makeshift bed, his chest wrapped in bandages.

Robert reached out to her. "Angelica. I was afraid for you."

She walked to him and took his hand. "Clay took me, but I escaped and I'm so glad you'll be all right. You're coming home with us when the doctor says we can take you."

The doctor listened to Robert's chest again. "Your lungs are clear and you can walk, though I wouldn't recommend being on your feet for any length of time. I want you on bed rest for the next ten days. Then you'll come back, and I'll remove the stitches, assuming you don't get an infection before then."

Robert frowned. "I won't, Doc. I refuse to have an infection."

The doctor chuckled. "I admire your conviction and I hope you're right." He turned to Angelica. "I've got a bottle of laudanum for you. Give him half-a-teaspoon in water every three hours. Normally, I'd say every four hours, but he's a big man. Rather than increasing the dose, I'm adjusting the time instead. Also, I want his bandages checked every day, cleaned and changed every two days. If there is any yellow seepage, I want him back here immediately. "

"I will, Doctor. I promise I won't let him hurt himself." *I hope I'm telling him the truth. What if Clay comes and Robert tries to protect me?*

Robert frowned at the doctor. "How's Angelica supposed to help me if I fall? She's too little."

She put her hands on her hips. "Ha. I'm stronger than I look."

Robert snorted. "How is a little bit like you gonna protect me? I'm the one to be protecting you."

She grinned and looked toward her husband. "Jared will teach me to shoot…won't you, dear?"

Jared lifted a brow.

Angelica was afraid he'd turn her down, but then the corner of his mouth twitched up.

He crossed his arms over his chest. "That's not a bad idea."

Robert shook his head. "She's got no business with a gun. She'll—"

Jared raised his hand, palm out toward Robert. "No. She has a point. First, she needs to be able to take care of herself when I'm not around. And second, Clay will never suspect that she knows how. I've got my deputies watching for Clay and Bill tracking him. He should be returning to town to give me the ransom demand. If you think you can manage for a few hours on your own, I'll take Angel out behind the house tomorrow."

"Can I manage on my own? 'Course I can. Think I'm a baby?" Robert grumbled.

Angelica walked over to Robert and kissed his forehead. "We all know you can take care of yourself, but I need to learn so I can protect myself for when you,

Jared and Ken aren't available to do so. I won't let Clay take me again."

"Did I hear my name?" Ken knocked on the open door.

Angelica turned toward her new friend. "You certainly did."

He smiled. "I hope it was in a good context."

"Oh, it was. Jared's teaching me how to shoot.."

Ken's eyebrows knitted together. "Are you sure that's necessary?"

Jared nodded. "I do. I don't want her to be at Stockton's mercy again."

Frowning, Ken walked to Robert's bedside and then turned toward Angelica. "Were you in danger? What have I missed?"

She explained what happened and why she wanted to learn to use a gun.

"I agree. She needs to learn, but I don't think she needs to carry a large gun. A derringer should be enough." Ken reached into his vest pocket and produced a small handgun. "Like this one."

Angelica walked to Ken. "May I hold it?"

"Certainly." Ken handed her the pistol.

She held it and marveled at its light weight. "I think this weapon would do very well." Angelica looked over at Jared. "I could put it in my skirt pocket and no one would be the wiser. Can I get one of these?"

He nodded. "I think that would work perfectly for

you. I have one, just like that at home. I'll take you out and teach you how to use it…safely."

She grinned at her husband. "Good."

Jared sighed. "I hope I'm doing the right thing. If you injure yourself, I don't know what I'll do."

She turned toward him. "It is trust me." *Now if I could just believe I can shoot Clay. What if I can't? What if he shoots me first because I have the gun?*

CHAPTER EIGHT

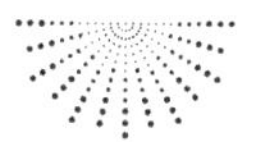

The next morning after the breakfast dishes were done, she and Jared walked west a few hundred yards out away from the house and town.

Jared didn't want there to be any accidents. And this way he was still available to the townsfolk, if needed.

Angelica and Jared left Ken with Robbie, in case Stockton showed up.

She noticed cans already set on several tree stomps. "You were prepared to teach me."

He shook his head and pulled a small gun from his coat pocket. "Actually, this is where I come to practice so I'm sharp when I need to use my weapon. Are you ready to learn?"

She rolled her shoulders and nodded. "More than ready."

"Then follow me."

Jared walked until they were about twenty feet from

the targets. “This is good. In order to do any real damage, this distance is as far away from Clay as you can be. Any farther and you might wound him but even then probably not badly.”

Angelica eyed the targets. “I seem awfully close. I’m not sure I want him that near to me. What if I miss?”

He looked at her and then handed her the gun. “Don’t.”

She blinked twice and swallowed hard. “Okay.” Then she set her jaw. “I won’t.”

“Hold out your hand flat holding the gun.”

She did. The gun was very small. It only filled her palm from heel to the middle of the middle finger. It had four barrels and even so, the weight wasn’t much. She could easily wield this weapon.

Jared held her palm with one hand and pointed to parts of the gun with the other. “This is a Sharps Pepper-box. It has four barrels, which means you have four shots.”

“Your gun only has one barrel, yet when you clean it you remove six bullets.”

“Good observation. The only reason I can think of is the manufacturer thought four barrels would give the most power and still keep its small size.”

“That doesn’t make much sense, but what do I know about guns?”

He grinned. “I know a lot about guns, and it doesn’t make sense to me, either.”

She laughed. "Good. I feel better now."

"Okay, I'll show you how to load and unload the gun. Rule number one. Never point a gun at someone unless you mean to use it. Understand?"

Angelica noted how serious he sounded and nodded. "Yes, I understand."

He quickly loaded four bullets into the gun's chamber and then just as fast unloaded it. Jared handed her the gun and the bullets. "Now, you try it."

She opened the chamber by sliding the barrel forward and loaded the bullets, then slid the chamber closed. Opening the gun again she took out each bullet and then grinned up at Jared.

He nodded. "Very good. Now, do it again. I want loading the weapon to become second nature to you so you can load it quickly, if necessary. You'll carry it loaded but if you expend all your bullets, you'll need to be able to load it."

"I understand." She stood there, loaded each bullet and then unloaded the gun…ten times.

"That's good. Let's get you used to firing the gun now. I want you to hold the gun at arm's length, but keep your elbow slightly bent. Don't keep your arm stiff or you'll hurt yourself."

Angelica tilted her head and wrinkled her brow. "How will I hurt myself?"

"The gun has a kick you're not used to or prepared for. Keeping your arms stiff can throw you off balance. You'll not only miss your target with the second bullet, you'll have wasted a shot and have no more room for error."

"Got it. Where do you want me to stand?"

"Right here. Put your legs apart to steady yourself. Okay, load the gun and look down the barrel to the piece of metal standing up at the end. It's called the sight. Center the sight on the can you want to hit. Then squeeze the trigger back slowly. Do not pull the trigger. You'll move the gun and miss your target, whether it's a can or a man."

Nodding, she concentrated on loading the gun. Her mouth was open and her tongue moved back and forth across her bottom lip. When she realized what she was doing, she stopped, clamping her mouth shut. Soon, she was back to holding her mouth open.

Jared used a single knuckle to lift her chin and shut her mouth. "Didn't your mama ever tell you you'd catch flies that way?"

She chuckled. "I sometimes open my mouth and lick my lips when I'm concentrating on something."

He just shook his head. "Okay, I want you to aim for the can on the left." Jared pointed toward the cans on the three stumps. "Just use the sight like I showed you."

She lifted the gun, aimed and squeezed the trigger. A loud boom sounded shaking her to her toes. "Oh, my gosh. The sound this little gun makes is loud."

"Yes, the gun makes a big noise for being so small. Let's go see what you did."

Angelica walked to the stump and looked down at the left target. “I missed it entirely.”

“Yes, you did, but you got the one in the middle.”

She looked again and sure enough, the center can was gone. Angelica gazed up at Jared.

He was grinning and then began laughing.

“Don’t laugh at me.” But she smiled and then laughed, too.

“For what it’s worth the left can moved…I think you scared it.”

She laughed harder and unable to catch her breath, she gulped for air.

“Okay, sweetheart, let’s try again.”

She nodded, powerless to say anything. *Did he really call me sweetheart?*

“Now, aim at your target. Center the sight on it. Squeeze the trigger and be sure to keep your eyes open.”

“Oh, dear. Did I close them last time? No wonder I didn’t hit the correct target.”

“You did, but this time, you’ll keep them open. I have faith in you.”

She nodded and aimed the gun. Forcing her eyes open, she squeezed the trigger slowly and fired. The stump on the left exploded out where she hit it.

“That’s better. Now I want you to aim a little higher, still keeping the can in your sight, but just the top of it instead of the center.”

“All right.” She lifted the pistol and aimed where he said.

The can fell over but not off the stump.

Jared looked at her and gently lowered her arm. Then he started toward the targets.

Angelica quickly followed.

He picked up the can and chuckled.

"Well?" She stepped closer. "Don't just stand there and laugh, let me see."

On the very bottom of the can was a bullet hole.

"All right. I take it you didn't mean to hit it so low."

She sighed. "No, I didn't but at least I hit it."

"That you did." He chuckled again. "A few more practice shots and we'll call it a day."

She nodded and then returned to the shooting area followed by Jared. When he was beside her, she turned and looked at the can. "You'll fall down this time, darn it, and with my bullet right through you."

Jared lifted a brow. "Now you're talking to the can? I hope it listens to you."

She aimed and fired.

The can fell, but wood splintered into the air from below it.

"Okay. Did you see that you're still hitting too low? Aim higher still, just a little. You don't want to overcorrect and miss the target altogether."

Angelica nodded, brought the pistol up, aimed and fired. The can toppled over. "Woohoo! It fell. Did you see it? It fell."

Jared took her in his arms. "I saw it and you were perfect. You kept your eyes open, arm straight and squeezed the trigger." He lowered his head and took her smiling lips with his.

As soon as he began to kiss her, she melted. She dropped the gun and wrapped her arms around his neck, kissing him back.

He broke the kiss and rested his forehead against hers. "I wish we were at home. I'd take you to bed and make love to you."

"No, you wouldn't. Robbie is there…remember?"

He groaned. "You'll have to learn to be quiet."

She leaned back and lifted a brow. "I'll have you know, I am quiet."

He chuckled. "If that is what you believe, then we're in trouble, darlin'."

She pushed away. "Am I really noisy?"

Jared nodded. "I'm grateful I can get your response, but we should probably refrain from lovemaking at home while Robbie is with us."

Sighing, she nodded. "Yes, I suppose we should."

Jared stooped and picked up the derringer she dropped, emptied the chambers and shoved the little gun in his pocket. "If we'd gone to the hills, I'd have made love to you on a nice soft bed of grass, but we're much too close to the house and town right now. Let's go back home. Robbie is probably awake now and wanting company."

"And I need to cook dinner for all of us. Will you come with me to the butcher? I need to get more meat if Robbie is eating with us. I want to get another pork roast and I don't want to go by myself."

He put an arm around her waist and started walking toward the house. "I don't want you going anywhere by yourself until I get Clay Stockton in custody. If he's not dead from you hitting him, he'll know his days as a free man are numbered. I want him to come back into town before he leaves for safer, greener pastures."

"If he's not dead, he knows I've told you all I know, so he may not come back here."

"That's a possibility. Let's face that when we find out if he's dead or not."

"What can I do to help?"

He put his hands on her shoulders. "Nothing. I want you to stay with Robbie. I don't want you hurt by a stray bullet or by one aimed at you."

Shivers ran up and down her spine. She knew Clay wouldn't hesitate to kill her now. Angelica knew where his safe house was and he'd admitted to her he'd killed the prostitute in Chicago and Vanessa here. Angelica knew his secrets. If he found her alone, she was as good as dead.

She nodded. "I'll stay with Robbie. Let's get the roast and head home."

Jared took them directly to the butcher.

Angelica picked out a three-pound boneless pork roast hoping it along with the four-pound roast at home, would be enough to feed herself and three big men. She'd never seen anyone eat as much as these men did.

Michael certainly hadn't. And cooking for her and Jared wasn't a very good indicator of how much food it would take to satisfy these men.

Angelica carried the roast in her left arm like it was a baby and held Jared's hand with her right as they walked home.

"While you're with Ken and Robbie…safe…I'll visit Judge Blackstone and give him the evidence on Clay. I don't want the cufflink to be in my hands because, no matter what happens to me, that will convict Clay."

She wrinkled her brows as she frowned. "How can a cufflink convict him?"

"He always wears them, or he did until after Vanessa's death. They have his initials on them. The jeweler always puts the customer's initials on them. And since they are diamond cufflinks he was always flashing them. They're very rare here in Virginia City."

"Then you better take it quickly. Tomorrow I can show you where his cabin is if you want?"

"I was just about to ask you for that exact information. As much as I hate for you to go anywhere near there again, if Bill hasn't found it, I don't have any choice."

She leaned against him, took his hand in hers and squeezed it gently. "As long as I'm with you, I'm safe."

He puffed out his chest. "I'm glad you feel that way, but I want you to carry your gun at all times…even if you're with me."

"All right. I can do that, but I hope I never have to use it."

"Once Clay is in custody, you can probably stop if it makes you feel uncomfortable."

"It's not that, I'm okay carrying it but I don't want to *have* to."

"I understand and I don't blame you."

"Let's just get home and I'll start dinner while you and Ken visit with Robbie." Her voice broke. "I'm so sorry he was nearly killed because of me."

Jared stopped walking and turned her to face him. "You did nothing to hurt Robbie. Nothing. It's Clay Stockton's fault…his deed to pay for, not yours."

"Down deep I know, but I just feel so bad Robbie is hurt."

"I know and so does he, but taking the blame for Clay's actions doesn't help anyone."

She knew he was right and nodded. "Okay. I won't blame myself anymore."

He smiled. "Let's go. I'm ready to be home."

"Me, too."

The short walk home was quiet. As was dinner and the rest of the evening.

Angelica was too tired to make small talk after they all had retired to the living room. "If you'll excuse me, gentlemen, I believe I'll retire for the evening."

Jared stood and went to her. "Are you all right?"

"I'm just tired. It's been a long, somewhat stressful day."

He nodded. "That it has. I'll be in soon."

As she left the room she heard Robbie. "Is she all right? Have you gotten her with child yet?"

She looked down at her stomach and laid her hands on it. Was she? When was her last menses? When she realized the date she knew she was late. She'd missed two cycles now. When they married she was due for her cycle the following week, but they never came. Then she missed the next one and now if she didn't have it next week, that would be three. Was she expecting? Could the doctor tell this early? She'd only be around seven weeks now, but she'd wait until after she missed again before talking to him. The time was probably too soon, but she knew in her heart that she was pregnant. Would Jared be happy, too?

CHAPTER NINE

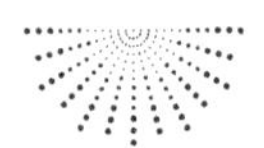

Angelica suddenly felt lighter of heart and practically skipped to their bedroom. She stripped off her clothes and stood sideways in front of the mirror. Was she? She sighed.

"What's the big sigh for?" Jared entered the room.

She was so occupied she hadn't heard him and jerked to cover herself. Taking a deep breath, she let it out slowly and lowered her arms. "You frightened me. I didn't hear you come in."

He grinned. "You wouldn't have heard an elephant herd come into the room. What were you so concentrated on? Not that I mind. I love seeing my wife with no clothes on."

"I heard Robbie's question."

He walked to the bed, sat, and took off his boots. "About getting you with child?"

She nodded. "That made me wonder…if I could be."

"And what did you decide?"

"It's possible." She dropped her nightgown over her head. "As long as Robbie is here, I'm wearing my nightgown to bed.

"Understood." He smiled. "Back to you expecting… isn't it too soon to tell?"

"Well, yes and no. I think I could be based on when I was expecting my menses." She stood by the bed. "This will be the third cycle I've missed."

"Can the doctor confirm your condition?"

She shook her head. "Probably not this early. We can ask Dr. Schossow when Robbie gets his stitches out. It will be almost two months we've been married by then."

He walked over to her and wrapped his arms around her waist. "Are you happy at the possibility?"

"I admit, I am. I've always wanted children. At first Michael and I didn't have time, because of his practice we barely saw each other, and then when I found out I was expecting, the shock of his death, took my baby from me, too."

"I'm sorry Angel. Truly, I am. But I'm glad you're here with me, and I want this baby very much, girl or boy."

She leaned back in his arms and put her hands on his chest. Hearing he wanted the baby, too, her heart felt full to bursting with joy. "I'm glad because I do, too. Girl or boy. Do you have names you want? Or is it too soon to know? I've always wanted a boy named James and a girl named Edwina."

"I like James for a boy. That's my middle name, remember?"

She giggled. "I can hardly remember my name from that ceremony. It's a blur, but since we agree on James that will be our son's name."

He laughed. "I know what you mean. As to a girl, I always wanted a daughter named Emma Rose."

She tilted her head. "That name is pretty, but my mother's name was Edwina. I really want to name my daughter after her."

"Then we will. James, if a boy and Edwina, if a girl. I'd also like to name the boy after Robbie, so James Robert. What do you think?" He kissed her neck.

She moved her head back and pushed her hands up his chest and then wrapped her arms around his neck. "I think it's perfect." Standing on tiptoe Angelica kissed him, really kissed him. She was happier than she'd been for a while, though she still wondered if he loved her. She put that notion out of her mind and kissed him with all her heart.

He lifted her in his arms and laid her in the middle of the bed. Jared removed his clothes and came down beside her. "I want to make love to you."

"I want that, too." She bit her lip remembering what he said about the noise she makes. "Are you sure we should with both Robbie and Ken here?"

"I'll make sure you're quiet…trust me."

She did.

Another ten days passed with no sight of Clay Stockton. She could see the way this event wore on Jared. He hardly ate and, when they went to bed, he was almost desperate to make love. That was the only time he seemed to relax, when he was in her arms, loving her.

Angelica didn't mind in the least. She wanted to soothe her husband. If she could figure out a way to help him she would. But the answer eluded her.

Today, Robbie was supposed to get his stitches out. She and Ken were going with him to make sure the doctor would actually take them out.

Angelica kept the stitches clean and dry. She checked every day for seepage and infection but never saw any.

Robbie was champing at the bit to get out of there and back to his own house.

The three of them stayed in the waiting room until the doctor called them. She passed the time with her knitting.

Ken read a book.

Robbie paced from one side of the room to the other.

She looked up from her knitting. "Robbie, you'll wear a hole in Dr. Schossow's carpet if you don't relax."

He nodded, but went back to pacing.

Finally, the doctor came into the waiting room. "Robert MacGregor, I'll see you now."

Angelica put her project away and stood.

Ken closed his book and also stood.

"There's no need for either of you to come back. I'll let you know if he needs further care."

"Very well. Thank you, Doctor," said Angelica.

Ken sat. "Yes, thanks Doc."

She sat again and continued working on a blanket for her baby. It was a full two months now since she and Jared were married and she was almost certain she was expecting. A thought occurred to her…perhaps she missed her menses because she was under too much stress, but she discounted that explanation because it wouldn't explain why she missed the second cycle.

Robbie and the doctor returned in about fifteen minutes.

"He's just fine now, Angelica. Robert can go home and take care of himself."

She smiled. "That's good. I'm glad Robbie is all right. Um, do you have a few minutes to see me, Doctor Schossow?"

The man with a kindly face smiled and nodded. "Of course, come on back."

She started to follow, but stopped and turned to Robbie and Ken. "You'll both wait for me won't you?"

Robbie settled his bulk into a chair. "Of course, take your time."

"Thank you, Robbie. I won't be long."

She went back to the surgery and closed the door behind her.

The doctor had his hands in his coat pockets. "What can I do for you, Angelica?"

She looked down for a moment, thinking what to say. "Well, I think I might be expecting but I've only been married for two months. Can you tell that soon?"

He leaned against the counter of the cupboard against one wall. "Not usually, but it depends on your menses. How many have you missed?"

Angelica's heart pounded in her chest. She was anxious and hoped he could give her a definitive answer, though she would have been surprised if he did. "Two and next week will be three, assuming it still doesn't arrive."

"You could have missed them because of all the stress you've been under, but if you miss them again, we can check you then. Let's wait for two more weeks and then I'll check you out. How's that sound?"

Her shoulders sagged a little. "Fine. Thank you, Doctor."

He moved to the door and opened it for her. "Anytime, my dear."

The men were right where she left them

Robbie looked up from a book he was reading when she approached.

Ken put down his book and stood. "Are you all right?"

She waved off his question. "Right as rain."

"All done?" asked Robbie.

"Yes." She looked toward Ken. "I just had a couple of questions and he answered them for me."

"Satisfactorily, I hope,"said Ken.

"Oh, yes. He did most certainly. You can take me home now, Robbie. Then if you want, you can stay for dinner. You probably don't have anything in the house to eat anyway and Jared will be back then, you can find out if he's made any headway."

Robbie put the book down and stood. "That's a good idea. Thank you for your kindness."

Ken opened the door for Angelica and Robbie, then followed them through and closed the door.

"You're a good man, Robbie MacGregor," she said in her best imitation of his burr." You help me all the time, coming with me to get my groceries and run my errands. The least I can do is serve you dinner."

Ken laughed.

Robbie blushed at her praise. "I'm glad I can be of help. I have even more reason to take care of Stockton now. Not only did he murder Vanessa, he almost murdered me and he kidnapped you. He has to pay."

She looked up at him. "He will. Jared won't let him get away with this. I told him where Clay's lodge is and he's determined. He will find him and bring him to justice."

"Jared better find him before I do. I'll give him justice…Highland justice."

Angelica stopped and placed a hand on his arm.

"Please, Robbie, let Jared handle it. I don't want to see you in jail."

He covered her hand with his. "I'll do my best to let Jared capture him to go before the judge. But if I run into him first, I'm not promising to control myself. I'll try, just for you, Angel. I'll try."

"That's all I ask." She turned and started walking again, but her heart was heavy. Jared had to get Clay into jail. He just had to.

Angelica finished her errands and the men walked her home. Her sense of foreboding didn't leave her, but she had to have faith in Jared. He wouldn't let his friend go to jail, if he could prevent it.

Robbie and Ken went through the house and made sure every window and door was locked.

"I'm going home with Robbie. I'll be back for dinner with him, too," said Ken.

She nodded. "See you both then." Angelica locked the door after them. She was alone and should be preparing dinner but just couldn't make herself do it. She sat on the sofa and thought about Clay Stockton. Where could he be hiding?

Jared came in the kitchen door. "Angel, I'm home."

She entered from the living room. "Jared. I'm so glad you're here. I'm worried about Robbie. He's determined to kill Clay Stockton, unless you capture him first." She walked into his waiting arms. "I don't want to see Robbie go to jail for murder." Tears formed in her eyes, and when she blinked, they ran down her cheeks like twin rivers in the forest.

"Shh, now. I'll take care of Robbie, and I won't let him go to jail. Trust me."

She gazed up at him, her eyes full of tears. "Thank you." Angelica pulled him down for a kiss.

He went easily, controlling the kiss, deepening it.

He was loving her with his mouth, and she loved him back.

Pulling back he placed his forehead against hers. "Feel better?"

"I always feel better when you kiss me."

"Good." He gave her a peck on the lips. "Now, I guess I better go find, Robbie, before he does something stupid."

"He's coming for dinner if that's any help."

"It is. I'll know where he is and not have to search for him. But I still have to find Clay. He's got to be somewhere in this town. I've got Bill watching the cabin…oh, right, the hunting lodge." Jared rolled his eyes.

She unwound her arms from around his neck and he left out the back door. Angelica felt bereft when he left her. She locked the door and went about her morning chores.

Today was laundry day, but that would have to wait

until Clay was found. She would not be outside alone until then.

She finished the dishes and opened the back door to throw the dirty water out.

"Hello, Angel. Bet you didn't expect to see me, huh?"

She screamed and dropped the pan.

Clay's voice was cold even if he was trying to sound friendly. She knew better.

Regaining her composure, she looked up at him and backed into the house. "What do you want, Clay? You should know from last time that Jared won't trade me. Besides the fact he's given the evidence to Judge Blackstone. He couldn't give it to you if he wanted to. And he doesn't."

He followed her and shut the kitchen door. Then moved to the sink and looked out the window, always keeping his gun directed at her. Finally, with his back to the stove, he stopped. "That's too bad. I really had hopes for you two having a long and happy marriage, but it doesn't look like that will happen." He lifted his gun to point at her.

She leveled her derringer in her pocket and squeezed the trigger, shooting straight through her skirt.

The bullet hit Clay in the right arm. His eyes went wide and he bared his teeth. "You little—"

Angelica quickly removed her derringer from her pocket and fired again.

This time, she hit him in the right leg and he fell to

his knees, dropping his gun.

She moved closer and pointed her weapon at Clay. "Do you want me to continue? I'm not a very good shot but I've been lucky so far. Maybe I will be with my next two shots, too. 'Though at this distance I could hardly miss."

He held up the hand that was not pressing on his leg wound. "Stop. Please. Stop. I don't want to die."

"I don't suppose Vanessa or Renee, that prostitute in Chicago, wanted to die, either, but you took that choice away from them. Why shouldn't I do the same to you?" She closed one eye and aimed down the top of the barrels.

"Because I won't let you," a stern voice sounded from behind her.

"Jared." Relief coursed through her and she lowered her gun as she turned to embrace him.

Clay took advantage, retrieved his revolver and shot at the two of them, hitting Angelica high in the back on her right side.

She fell to the floor.

A roar sounded from outside and Robbie barreled through the door. He picked up Clay and shook him until Clay's gun hit the floor. Then he threw him through the opening where the door used to be.

Robbie turned to Jared. "I'll take him to jail. I promised Angel I wouldn't kill him. You get her to the doc's."

Jared nodded, picked her up and headed out the

kitchen door..

"Oh, God, that hurts."

"Angel, don't talk. Save your energy."

She laughed. "God, it hurts so much."

Jared smiled down at her. "I know it does, sweetheart. I'm hurrying."

He looked pale and scared.

"Jared, I'll be fine—" The probability that she was expecting hit her. What if this wound made her lose another baby? Her eyes filled with tears. "What if…what if—"

"Shh." he said. "We'll deal with that when the time comes.".

Could he read her mind?

"You don't know for sure. You said yourself it was too early to know if you're with child."

She felt him start to walk faster. "Jared, is there something I don't know about?" Every bump and bounce in his arms hurt. She gritted her teeth and tried not to make noise. She could only imagine what he must be thinking with the faces she made.

"Only another block and we'll be there. You'll be fine, Angelica."

"Angelica? Am I dying? Is that why you don't call me Angel?" *I'm dying. I'll never see my baby.*

"No, no sweetheart, you're not dying. You couldn't talk this much if you were dying. Trust me."

"I always do." She closed her eyes and the world went black.

CHAPTER TEN

Angelica had passed out.

Jared was just as happy she had because now he could run and not worry about hurting her. He approached the door to Doctor Schossow's clinic and pounded on the door with his boot.

"Just a minute. I'm coming. Hold your horses, will you?"

Mabel Schossow opened the door, took one look at Angelica and ushered Jared inside. "Follow me back to the surgery. I'll get Lyle. What happened?"

"Clay Stockton shot her. He was probably aiming for me but he could have been aiming for her. She knows a lot that will come out at his trial. He might have been trying to prevent her from testifying."

Mabel's back stiffened as she hurried to the operating room. "Never had any use for Clay Stockton. Who do you think had to patch up those girls after he got done with them? Lyle did. Clay had never killed one before but the battering Vanessa took was typical for the way he treated those women."

Jared followed the doctor's wife into the surgery, called such because all of his operations, big and small, occurred in this room.

"Lay her there on the table, while I get Lyle."

"I'm here, Mabel," said the doctor from the doorway. "I need to wash my hands and instruments."

"I'll leave you to it." Mabel left the room.

Jared stood by the table Angel lay upon. "Doc, why didn't you ever report him?"

"The girls wouldn't let me. Said they wouldn't get paid if Smitty or Clay went to jail."

"Well, I wish I'd known. We might have saved a life if I'd known."

The doctor washed each implement with lye soap and then rinsed them with alcohol.

"I don't want her to get an infection." He looked at Angelica, shook his head and frowned. "Shot her in the back. Figures. A person like him can't even be called a man. He's an animal. Who took him to jail…I'm assuming he's in jail?"

"Robert MacGregor."

The doctor grinned. "Good. I know his feelings toward Clay Stockton, and Stockton will be the worst for it."

"Angelica shot him twice before Robbie took him to jail."

Doctor Schossow's smile widen as he began to dry his hands. "Did she, now? Good for her. Take off her blouse, please, Jared. I need to see what kind of injury we're looking at."

Jared did as requested, sickened by the blood soaked garment. "Doc, as you know, she was fairly sure she was expecting and wondered if this would affect that."

Doc examined the entrance of the bullet, on her shoulder. "Well, the wound itself is nowhere near that part of the body, so it shouldn't be a problem. The problem will be if her body decides it can't keep the baby."

Jared had to look away. He was so glad she was unconscious for this examination. "Would she be far enough along for you to confirm or not that she's with child?"

The doctor probed the wound with his finger. The bullet didn't come out the front, so it was in her shoulder…somewhere. "Not yet. I told her we need to wait another two weeks before I can examine her and tell."

He kept his eyes averted. Jared could watch a criminal with a wound squirm and cry when Doc probed the wound, but not Angelica, not his Angel.

"I'm surprised you know so much. Most husbands wouldn't have a clue what I was talking about."

Jared shrugged. "We talk about a lot of things, and when she thought she might be pregnant, she told me why. She's an amazing woman. I can't lose her."

Doctor Schossow, stopped his probing and looked

directly at Jared. "You've fallen in love. Have you told her yet?"

"Fallen in love…nah…I couldn't…could I?" He thought about it for several moments. "I guess I am. I never realized. We were too busy just being married and then she got kidnapped by Clay."

The doctor stared over the rim of his glasses. "I should have checked her out after that event…just to make sure she was healthy and not in need of someone to talk to."

Jared raised his chin. "Angel talked to me. If I thought she needed more help, I'd have come to you."

The doctor nodded. "I'm glad she could talk to you. Now, let's get this bullet out so you can get her home and into bed." He took a long pair of tweezers and put them into her wound, moving them around to find the bullet.

Jared stared at Angel's face again, thankful she was unconscious. She was so beautiful and looked like she was sleeping. He had to look away.

Anger hit him like a brick wall. Clay had nearly killed her. Jared was tempted to take the law into his own hands and deal with Clay like he deserved, but that's not what Angel wanted, so he tamped down those feelings and concentrated on her.

At last the bullet hitting the metal basin sounded loudly in the otherwise quiet room.

"There we go. Now, I'll put some alcohol in there to

stave off infection and sew her up. I'm glad she won't feel this part. It's the worst."

"More so than digging around in her back for the bullet?"

"'Fraid so."

He walked over to the cabinet, took out a clear bottle and brought it back to the table. "Hold her down. Just in case she awakes."

Jared held her shoulders, putting enough pressure on them so she couldn't turn over.

The doctor poured the liquid into the wound, then blotted it with a towel before stitching it up.

"I've given her extra stitches in the hopes she won't break them loose. You can dress her now. Here is a clean surgical gown you can put on her."

Jared turned Angel over and put the garment on, careful to hold her gently and not disturb the new injury.

"You'll have to keep her in bed for the next week. By then the wound should be healed enough for me to take out the stitches. Treat her like she did Robbie. I'll give you some willow bark tea which should help eliminate the fever if she gets one."

"If anything else happens, send someone for me." He went back to the cabinet, this time returning with a small brown bottle. "This is laudanum. See that she gets a full teaspoon in water when she wakes and half a teaspoon every four hours after that. She'll sleep most of the time for the first few days. On about the third day, you can decrease the laudanum to every six hours and see how she tolerates the pain." He handed Jared the bottle. "If she does well, then decrease it again to three times a day. I want to wean her off of it. It's very addictive."

Jared put the bottle in his back pants pocket so it wouldn't poke Angel on the way home. He would have to see if Bill would take care of filing the paperwork with Judge Blackstone while he stayed home with Angel. The thought of not being there when she woke was abhorrent.

"Oh, Doc, would you go to the jail and take care of Clay Stockton's wounds?"

"I'll go, but I'm making sure he feels every stitch for treating those women that way."

"Good for you, Doc. If there was a way I could arrest Smitty, I would, believe me." Jared carefully picked up Angel, cradling her in his arms. "If you'll get the doors for me, I'd appreciate it."

The doctor opened the door and Jared headed out.

In the waiting room waited Robbie and Ken.

Robbie stood first. "How is our Angel?"

"Yes," echoed Ken. "How is she? Will she be all right?"

Jared was so touched that his friends were Angel's friends, too. "She'll be fine. She has to stay in bed for a week but after that she'll be right as rain."

"If you need any help caring for her, you let me know," said Robbie. "She took care of me when I was shot, I'd be grateful to do the same for her."

A lump formed in Jared's throat, making it hard to talk. "Thank you. Thank you both," he looked at Ken, "for being here for her."

Ken opened the door. When Jared was about to walk through it, he clapped him on the shoulder. "We love her, too."

That word again. Love. *How could I not have realized I love her? I don't think I could survive if something happened to her.*

He looked down into her lovely face. *I was a fool to think I could remain aloof and not fall in love with her. I guess I never thought it would happen to me. I was a fool.*

Jared walked home with Ken and Robbie on either side of him.

"If you'll give me your key, I'll open the door," said Robbie.

"You'll have to get it Ken, I can't while holding her. It's in my right vest pocket.

Ken got the key and handed it to Robbie.

Walking ahead of Jared, Robbie unlocked the front door and held it open.

Jared stopped in the living room and looked at his friends. "Would you make some coffee, please, and put on a kettle of water, too? The doctor gave me some tea to give her in case she gets a fever, so I want a kettle hot all the time."

"Sure, I'll do the coffee and Ken can do the kettle,"

said Robbie. He nodded at Ken, pointing toward the kitchen.

"You can count on us for whatever you need," said Ken.

"Thank you." Jared carried her straight to the bedroom, laid her on the bed and removed her clothes, put on her nightgown and turned down the blankets from underneath her, lifting her to the other side of the bed and then picked her up, turned down the blankets on this side. Then placed her between the sheets and covered her. He gently pushed her lank hair off her forehead and behind her ear. "I'm so sorry, sweetheart. So very sorry."

"Nothing to be sorry for."

Jared nearly jumped out of his boots. "How long have you been awake?"

"Since you brought me in here and undressed me." She moved and then groaned. "I don't feel very well right now. I seem to remember being shot. Did you shoot him back? Did you kill Clay?"

"No. Robert took him to jail. Remember?"

She blinked several times. "Yes, yes, I remember now. You were taking me to Doc's."

He took the laudanum from his back pocket and set it on the nightstand. Then he sat gingerly on the side of the bed next to her and took her hand in his. "Doc got the bullet out and sewed you up. I've got laudanum to give you. It will help with the pain so you can sleep and heal."

She laughed softly. “I remember giving it to Robbie. He didn’t like it much but got used to it. He was also glad to be off of it. I guess I’ll feel the same way, though I would like some now. I’m hurting ever so much.” She scrunched her eyes shut.

He knew she was trying to get through a wave of pain. Jared went to the commode and poured a half glass of water from the pitcher. Then he added a full teaspoon of the medicine like the doctor told him to. He hoped she’d get some rest.

Jared took the glass to her and helped her sit up enough to drink it.

“Robbie was right. That stuff is nasty. It better work or I’m not taking it.”

He chuckled. “Oh, it will work, just give it a chance. Now, would you like me to fix you something to eat? We’ve got some chicken broth you canned in the pantry. I can heat you up a bowl?”

She shook her head. “I’m really not up to eating anything. Maybe just a cup of tea.”

“Coming right up. You’ve got a couple of admirers who’d like to see you and make sure I’m taking good care of you. If either of them think I’m not, they’ll both mop the floor with me.”

She lifted her hand to him.

He took hers with both of his.

“You’re taking very good care of me. What did the doctor say about the baby?”

“It’s too soon to tell, but if you are pregnant, this

injury shouldn't have any effect. We just need to keep you calm and healing. I don't want you to worry about anything. Stockton is in jail, and Doc was headed over to treat the gunshot wounds you inflicted." He laughed. "Doc's looking forward to inflicting a little pain of his own when he stitches Clay up."

Angel laughed a little then squeezed her eyes shut and grimaced. "Don't make me laugh. It hurts too much."

"I'm sorry, sweetheart. I'll be more thoughtful."

She gazed up at him, wide-eyed.

"What's the matter, sweetheart? You look like you've seen a ghost."

"Maybe I have. Who are you, and what have you done with my husband?"

He lifted his brows, then looked behind him. "Who are you talking to?"

"You. You called me sweetheart, twice in a row. Are you well?"

Jared chuckled, his heart light. "I like the name sweetheart. It fits you. You're my sweetheart and no one else's." He leaned down and kissed her lips. "Now I'm leaving to get you that tea. You just close your eyes and relax. I'll be back shortly."

"All right. It's not like I'm going anywhere."

Jared left the room smiling.

In the kitchen, Ken and Robbie sat at the table, each with a cup of coffee.

"Is she okay?" asked Ken.

"Can we see her?" asked Robbie.

"Can we do anything for her?" asked Ken.

"Anything she wants, she's got it," said Robbie.

Jared lifted his hands, palms out. "Okay. Let me talk."

"So talk, already." Robbie held his fist on the table.

"She's feeling very sore. I gave her some laudanum and now she wants tea. I figure she'll be asleep by the time I get back, but you two can come and see her for yourselves."

Jared prepared a cup of tea. He added a little cold water to it in case she was awake and wanted to drink it right away. He didn't want it to be too hot. He carried the cup and headed back upstairs.

Ken and Robbie followed.

When they arrived at the bedroom, Angelica had her eyes shut.

Ken sighed.

"We'll come back later to see her," said Robbie.

"You'll do no such thing," said Angel. "I'm awake and expecting to see my friends. How are you, gentlemen?"

Ken and Robbie looked at each other and then back at Angel.

"We thought you were sleepin'." Robbie stepped up to the bed and took her hand. "We don't want you stayin' awake just for the sorry likes of us."

"There is nothing sorry about the likes of either of

you gentlemen. Now, tell me, you took Clay to the jail, right?"

"Right." Robbie looked away.

She squeezed his hand. "How was he when you got him to jail?"

"Alive."

She rolled her eyes. "I figured he would be."

Jared stood at the end of the bed and laughed at Robbie's attempt to stay in Angel's good graces.

"Ah, tell her," said Ken. "She'll find out, anyway."

Robbie reddened. "All right, I admit his face might have hit the dirt road a couple of times and he might have been slow to get his face off the dirt when he fell, But he was still alive and cussin' me out when I got him into the jail cell. Bill has the keys and I made him promise he wouldn't arrange an escape so he could shoot Stockton, though that's exactly what every man in this room would like to do."

Jared frowned. *Bill would never break the law any more than I would.*

When neither Ken nor Jared agreed, Robbie folded his arms over his massive chest. "Fine. I'm the only one who wanted to…and did…wipe that smile off that bas—"

"Robbie, name calling is beneath you," said Angel.

Robbie shook his head. "If you say so. Anyway, I did wipe the smile, and part of his nose, off his face. He won't be the pretty boy anymore."

Angel sighed. "I'm tired, my friends. Thank you for coming to see me, but now I need to sleep."

Jared straightened away from the end of the bed. "Okay, you heard the lady. Visiting hours are over. I'll be down after she goes to sleep."

Robbie kissed her on the forehead. "Get better, Angel."

Ken also kissed her forehead and muttered, "I think we'll play chess in a couple of days when you're better. Do you know how?"

She smiled. "I don't, but you can teach me, then I'll play with Jared."

Jared shook his head. "I'm a lousy chess player. Aren't I, Ken?"

Ken laughed. "You are. That's why I'm teaching her not you."

Jared pouted and then laughed. He looked at Angel, and she was smiling without a grimace, so her pain must be lessening, or at least becoming manageable.

The other two men left the bedroom.

Jared pulled the rocking chair up to the bedside and sat. He made it close enough that he could take Angel's hand in his. "I want you to get well quickly, so you'll follow the doctor's orders to the letter, right?"

"Of course," she answered.

He noticed she didn't look at him, so he figured she was keeping her options open. Robbie had gone crazy the last couple of days he was supposed to be on bed rest.

Jared would make sure she stayed in bed if he had to get in the bed with her.

Her eyelids were heavy and she tried to keep them open.

"Don't fight the sleep. You need it to heal."

"But I'll miss so much."

"I'll fill you in on anything that happens you should know about."

"I want to know what happens to Clay. What did Judge Blackstone say when you told him you'd captured Clay?"

Jared ran a hand behind his neck. "I haven't seen the judge yet. I'll do that after I make sure you sleep."

She promptly closed her eyes.

"Faking it doesn't count."

"You can leave now. What else can I do except go to sleep. Check on me when you return. I'll bet you I'm sleeping."

"I don't know if I'm comfortable with that arrangement."

Her words were slurring. "Gwan. Ifn I awake you tell me. Ken and Robbie here. I'n fine."

He furrowed his brows. "I don't know—"

She scooted him with her good arm. "Pwease."

"All right but I'll be right back. I'm sending Ken and Robbie in here in case you need something."

"That's not necessary. I'm turning on my side so I can get off the wound and going to sleep. Now."

He stood, bent down and kissed her. "See you in a few minutes."

"Okay."

Jared left the room.

What if the judge said the cufflink wasn't enough to keep Clay locked up? What if he tried to kill her again?

Angelica thought he'd never leave. The laudanum didn't seem to be working very much. It definitely didn't make the pain go away. She turned over, tears in her eyes. What if she was already pregnant? What if she lost this one, too?

CHAPTER ELEVEN

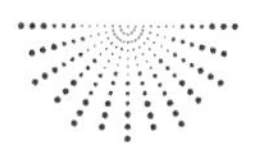

Angelica felt someone lightly rubbing her arm. She opened her eyes and turned over. She kicked off the covers. Hot. She was so hot.

"Jared?"

"Hi, sweetheart, you're awfully warm. I'll get some cool water and rub you down. Can you hear me, Angel?"

She saw his lips moving, but his voice was muffled like she had cotton in her ears. *What's the matter with me?*

Eyes wide, she grabbed Jared's arm. "I can't hear you. Why can't I hear you?"

He covered her hand with his. "You've got a fever. I think your lack of hearing is caused by it. I'll be right back."

He walked to the commode got a washcloth from the top drawer. Then he poured water into the basin and added the washcloth. He closed the bedroom door before returning to her.

"Let me help you out of your nightgown."

Angelica nodded and tried to sit up. A sharp pain made her cry out and fall to the mattress.

"Don't move. I'll move you. I don't want you to do it on your own." He bunched the hem of her nightgown around her waist, and then lifted her to a sitting position and removed the gown before laying her back down.

"Okay, let's get that fever down." He dipped the washcloth in the water and wrung it out. Then he started with her chest and neck.

The coolness felt wonderful. She closed her eyes and let him work.

"I need to get more water, and I'll make you a cup of the willow bark tea. I'll be right back." He pulled the sheet over her. "I'll tell our friends that you're not seeing visitors but you should still be covered until I return."

Still unable to hear him, she got the gist of what he said by reading his lips and nodded.

Angelica closed her eyes and must have nodded off. The next thing she knew, Jared was rubbing a cool cloth down her arms and legs, then up her torso to her neck and then her face. It felt so good, though she knew the fever still raged in her body.

"Here's your tea. Be careful, it's still warm. Here, let me sit you up.

Accepting his help, she sat on the edge of the bed and drank her tea.

Jared wiped the cool cloth up and down her back.

When she finished the tea, he helped her lie back down and began to rub her all over again.

Her eyes felt so heavy, she closed them, just for a moment. So sleepy.

When next she awoke, there was a heavy arm over her waist and a leg over her legs effectively cocooning her.

"Jared?"

"Yes, sweetheart. I'm here."

"Why are you in bed with me…naked?"

"Your fever broke and chills set in. I needed to warm you quickly and this is the fastest way to do it." He kissed her shoulder above her injury. "Don't worry, you're safe with me."

"I know I am, but I'm so sleepy."

"That's the laudanum. The willow bark tea was a long time ago, so I gave you laudanum this time."

"Oh, that was nice of you. I love you." *Was this too soon? Am I risking too much? Am I expecting too much from him? What if he's not ready to love me back?*

Angelica awoke alone. Had she imagined Jared was naked in bed with her? Did she imagine that she said *I love you*? She must have. But it seemed so real. She shook her head. Just a vivid dream, one she hoped she'd dream again and soon.

Pushing herself up to a sitting position took all of her strength. She moaned, unable to keep the sound inside. She had to sit there and just breathe through the pain. Had it been four hours yet? Surely it had been. Picking up the laudanum bottle she grabbed the spoon.

"What are you doing, sweetheart?"

"I hurt. I was taking more medicine. Can I? Has it been four hours yet?"

He hurried to her side. "I was coming to see if you were awake and ready for the next dose. I take it you are."

She sighed, her breath shallow. "Yes, please. I hurt so bad." A tear escaped and tracked down her cheek.

He prepared the laudanum for her. "Here you go. Do you want to lie back down after you drink it?"

Angelica took the glass and shook her head. "I need to sit up for a while. I feel like I've been in bed for days." She drank every drop of the medicine.

He took the empty glass and set it on the bureau then sat next to her and put an arm around her shoulders. "Actually, you have. Between the fever and the chills three days have passed. I even had Doc come see you. But he said I was doing everything right."

"Three days! Oh, my gosh, no wonder I feel like a rag doll. I need a bath."

Jared shook his head. "Sorry, darlin'. No getting that

injury wet. I can give you a bath in here with warm water and a washcloth. How's that sound?"

She suddenly realized he was fully dressed. *Just proof that my dream was just that...a dream.* "Yes, please. Anything is better than I am now. I don't know how you manage to sit next to me."

"Darlin' you can't do anything that would keep me away from you."

Angelica looked up into his dark blue eyes and saw the truth there. He would stay with her regardless of how she smelled or looked. "Kiss me. Then we'll see about the bath."

He gave her a light kiss on the lips and then a peck on the forehead.

"No. Really kiss me."

Jared grinned. He put both arms around her, careful of her wound, and kissed her deeply.

She could almost feel the love coming off of him, but that was just a dream. A beautiful, heavenly dream.

He caressed her jaw with a hand, kissed her closed eyes and her lips again. Jared was so gentle, caring. Her heart was near to bursting with love for the man.

"You've been up enough. I'll give you your bath. Wait just a moment until I can get warm water. Oh, you need to cover up. The gentlemen are champing at the bit to see you."

"They are both so sweet. You have nice friends."

He pushed her hair behind her ears. "Correction. *We*

have nice friends. They are yours now as much as they are mine."

She smiled and kissed his "Thank you for sharing your friends with me."

Jared chuckled. "I think now it's the other way around. They love you, too."

She leaned against him, ignoring the pain. She wanted the touch too much to stop. She soaked in his scent. Angelica loved the way he smelled. Sandalwood was her favorite scent for a man. Michael had worn it for her. She didn't even have to ask Jared. He'd already chosen the scent as his own.

"You need to lie down now. Come on."

She sighed and sat up straight before letting Jared help her to lie back on the mattress.

"That's my girl." He covered her with the blankets. "I'll tell them they can come in for just a moment, if you think you can handle it."

"I'd really rather have that bath first. I feel so grubby."

"That's fine. I'll just tell them you'll see them tomorrow when you're feeling better. How's that?"

She nodded, grateful she wouldn't have to paste on a smile and pretend she was feeling better than she was.

"I'll be right back with that water. Do you want to use your rose or lilac soap?"

"Rose, please."

"You got it."

She tried to take a deep breath, but the movement hurt her shoulder and she groaned.

Jared turned back. "What's the matter? Are you in pain? Do you want to put off your bath until later, after the laudanum has started working?"

"No, I want the bath but may I have a glass of water, please?"

"Sure." He went and filled up the glass.

She gulped this one down. "I think I best stop. I don't want to have to relieve myself right now. It hurts too much to get out of bed."

"Understood. Can I get you anything else before I go?"

"No, thank you. I'm ready for my bath now."

Jared left.

Angelica tried to breathe through the pain. Why was getting shot so painful?

A few minutes later, Jared returned with the tea kettle and a cup.

"What's in the cup?"

"Just tea. It will help soothe you."

"Thank you."

He set the cup on the nightstand. Then he went to the commode and poured water from the tea kettle into the basin. He followed that with cool water from the pitcher. Jared finally returned to the bed with the basin and two washcloths. One to wash her with and one to rinse her with. He started with her face and worked his way down to her feet. He even sat her up so he could wash her back below the bandage.

When the bath ended she sighed. "I feel so much better. Thank you. I feel positively wonderful. Even my shoulder isn't hurting now."

"That's great." He sat on the side of the bed. "Are you hungry?"

"Famished. What do we have to eat?"

"I can make you a roast pork sandwich. I bought bread at the bakery and Ken, Robbie and I had roasted pork for dinner. There's enough left for a sandwich or two."

She laughed and then grimaced. "I must remember not to do that. As to dinner, one sandwich will do nicely."

"Coming right up."

He's being so good to me. Does his care mean he loves me? He's called me sweetheart and darlin' and his girl. Do those pet names mean he loves me? I need to ask him if my dream was real. I really have to know because not knowing is driving me crazy.

CHAPTER TWELVE

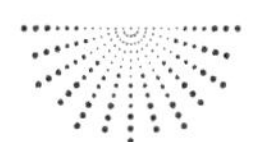

Angelica recovered quickly. When day seven came and she could get her stitches out, she paced the bedroom, dressed and ready to go.

Jared still lay in bed.

"Angel, I know you're anxious, but Doc isn't even awake yet. It's only six o'clock in the morning."

"I know, but I can't seem to calm myself. I want these stitches out so badly, I can't think of anything else. Except maybe about the trial. It starts tomorrow, right?"

Jared lay with his arm behind his head. "Yes. Judge Blackstone will be seating the jury tomorrow morning, and you'll need to testify tomorrow afternoon. Clay Stockton will finally pay for the murders he's committed and for shooting you. He'll hang."

She sat on the bed next to him. "As he should. Before we go to the doctor, I have to know if it was real or if I was dreaming. Did you warm me with your body when I had the chills?"

"Yes, I did. I wondered if you'd remember."

Her heart pounded in her chest and her hands shook, so she clutched the folds of her skirt. "Did I tell you I loved you?"

He smiled and nodded. "Yes, you did."

"Oh. I hadn't meant to tell you. I don't want you to feel obligated to say it back to me."

He sat up in bed, the blankets bunching at his waist. He patted the bed next to him.

She angled her body toward him.

"First, I will never say something because I feel obligated to. Next, I did put my arms and legs over and around you so I could get as much of us touching as possible. You were so cold your teeth were chattering. And last, but most importantly, I love you, very much. You are my Angel."

Tears filled her eyes and streamed down her cheeks. "I was so sure I dreamed the whole thing. I love you, too."

Jared took her in his arms and kissed her through all the tears she continued to shed. "Now, stop those tears, though I hope they're happy tears."

She nodded fast and laughed. "I feel silly, but you know what? I'm so relieved to finally have our feelings for each other out in the open. I don't want to hide my love any longer."

"Nor do I. You really are my angel. I feel like I only started to live when you came into my life."

"I didn't think I could love again, but you showed me I could. I could love and have children." She put her hands on her stomach. "I'm pretty sure I'm expecting. I feel changes in my body, inside and out. I can see where my stomach has a little bump and my breasts—"

He grinned. "I know. I feel the change there, too."

She kept her hands on her stomach. "I can't wait to be a mother, and I think you'll be a wonderful father. I'm so looking forward to this baby, and I already love it."

He placed a hand over hers where it rested on her belly. "I do, too." Jared pulled her into another kiss. When they broke apart he gave her a kiss on the nose. "I guess I might as well get up. We need to eat breakfast before we go to the doctor's office anyway."

"I'll go start the coffee."

When she heard Jared enter the kitchen, Angelica was almost done scrambling eggs for the three of them. Bacon sizzled in another skillet and biscuits were baking.

Jared joined Ken at the table. "What are your plans now that Stockton is in jail?"

Angelica brought him a cup of coffee.

"Thanks, Angel."

"You're welcome." She went back to the stove, stirred the eggs, drained the bacon, and removed the drop biscuits from the oven, while listening to the conversation.

"Wait around for the trial and make sure he's hanged."

"And then?"

Ken leaned back in his chair. "I don't know. Go back to Chicago I guess." A frown crossed his face. "Though I don't think I'll be a good Pinkerton. I've seen you do too much work for actual justice to go around being the bad man. I think I'll head west. After I sell everything in Chicago, I think I'll take the Oregon trail to Oregon City or before. Maybe I'll find a little town like this one and become the marshal there."

Jared took a sip of his coffee. "Or you could become my deputy. Virginia City is growing too fast for my current deputies and me to handle. There are just twenty-five of us and did you see the construction that is happening. Thousands of people will be coming here. I need someone, actually several someones, fulltime. My last fulltime deputy left to follow the gold. I've been told they were still bringing it up in Colorado Territory."

Ken lifted his brows just a bit and narrowed his eyes. "You really want me to be your deputy? You're not just offering to get me to stay?"

Jared shrugged. "That's part of it, but I know you'd make a good second chief deputy and just like for Bill, the town provides a wage and a house to live in now that John is gone."

"What kind of house would I be living in?"

Angelica returned to the table with plates of eggs, bacon and drop biscuits for the three of them and sat on Jared's right, across from Ken. "I can answer that. I've been by there. It's the cutest house. They've…well, actually, I've kept up the garden out front. I like being outside. Anyway, it's small, only has one bedroom, living room and kitchen. I think you'd be happy there even when you marry. It's only two houses down from this one toward town."

"Oh, no." He waved his hands in front of him. "I'm not getting married. Jared might have gotten lucky with you, but I'm not ready to marry. Even if I was I'm afraid to try the mail-order bride route. I'd probably get hairy Harriett, not an angel like you."

Her face heated. "Thank you for the compliment, but you don't know that for sure."

"Oh, yes I do. I'm not that lucky, believe me." He turned to Jared. "Back me up here."

Jared shook his head. "Can't do it. If my Angel thinks you'd find a good woman the way I did, then I agree."

Ken's shoulders slumped and he rolled his eyes. "I'll think about it. Let's change the subject. Don't you get your stitches out today?" he asked Angelica.

She grinned. "I certainly do and I can't wait. These are driving me crazy and I want to get back to doing my chores. I'm not used to being a lady of leisure. Just preparing breakfast this morning has been wonderful."

Jared reached over and squeezed her hand. "I don't know, I think you should be a lady of leisure."

Angelica shook her head. "I don't ever want that lifestyle. I like cleaning my house and cooking and soon, I hope, taking care of children. I don't want anyone else doing that for me."

Ken looked at Jared. "You definitely got the cream of the crop."

Jared gazed at her.

She saw the love in his eyes.

How long had the love been there and she overlooked it?

He took her hand and kissed it. "Yes, I did. I don't deny it."

Angelica pulled back her hand and finished the last bite of eggs so she didn't have to respond. Did he see the love in her eyes like she did his?

She finished her breakfast and looked up to see she was the last one to do so.

"I'll wash the dishes when I get back. Let's get to Doc's and have these stitches out. I want to be the first one there, so we don't have to wait."

Jared chuckled.

Ken laughed.

She widened her eyes. "What?"

"Only you would be excited to go to the doctor's. Everyone else dreads it," said Jared.

"I like Doctor Schossow. He's nice, and he'll let me go back to work."

"Don't get your hopes too high, sweetheart. He'll probably restrict you for a while so the wound will heal completely."

She sniffed the air. "We'll see. Let's go." She stood. "We'll be back shortly, Ken. Enjoy your coffee. Or maybe go for a walk and look at that house. Wouldn't it be nice to have a home?"

"I have a home in Chicago. I'd have to sell everything and ship it here. I don't know."

She walked around the table and set her hand on his shoulder. "But are you happy there? Think about it."

Jared waved her to leave. "Let's go sweetheart. I need to get to work, since I don't have a deputy that can handle everything…like Robbie, if he shows up at the jail."

Ken put up his hands. "All right. I'll check it out and give you my answer after I return."

Angelica clapped and put her hands together in front of her. "I know you'll make the right decision."

Ken nodded and took a sip of coffee.

What he had in his cup had to be cold, but she needed to go. "I'm ready."

Jared held out her shawl to her. "Let's go and get those out. I wouldn't mind having my wife back, too."

She donned the warm covering. October mornings were rather chilly. Angelica waved at Ken as Jared ushered her out the door.

Angelica and Jared walked the seven blocks to the doctor's office. The morning was lovely, just a little chill in the bright sunlight. The sky was so blue the white clouds seemed to pop out from it.

She pulled her shawl a little closer to her neck. "Thank you for getting me my shawl. I need it."

"Come here." Jared put an arm around her shoulders and pulled her close. "I'll keep you warm."

Angelica leaned against his hard body and he infused her with his warmth. She smiled up at him. "Thank you. This helps a lot."

"You're welcome. I love having you in my arms, anytime."

She loved being held by him. He always made her feel safe. Angelica knew that Stockton being in jail had a lot to do with the feeling, too.

"It's been nice walking with you like this. Thank you for keeping me warm."

"Anytime, my love."

She smiled up at him. "I love you, too."

He squeezed her to him.

They'd reached the doctor's office.

Jared kissed the top of her head before removing his arm. Then he knocked on the door.

Mabel Schossow answered the door. "Come, in. Come, in. Lyle said you'd be early, he's waiting to take your stitches out." The tall, round woman's light brown hair shone gold in the sunlight. "I'll take you back. He's waiting for you."

"Thank you," said Angelica. "I'm so ready to have them out. They are itching like crazy."

The woman laughed. “They always do and I guess the location of yours makes it even worse as they are hard to scratch and you don’t want to disturb the stitches, anyway. Ah, here we are.” Mabel opened the door.

Angelica saw Doctor Schossow leaning against the counter in the room. “Come in, Angelica. Take off your blouse and we’ll remove those stitches.”

She hopped up on the table and removed her blouse.

Jared leaned against the wall opposite the table with his arms crossed.

Doc walked over with a pair of scissors. He snipped and pulled each of the twelve stitches he’d used, finishing quickly.

She felt each stitch as it was removed. There wasn’t pain, just a twinge letting her know the stitch was gone.

Doc finished. “There you’re all set. You can dress.”

Angelica donned her blouse. “Thanks, Doc. I feel ever so much better. At least I don’t have to have Jared scratch my shoulder anymore.”

Jared pushed away from the wall. “I’ll have you know that I like scratching your shoulder or back or anywhere else you itch.”

She felt her face heat, and knew she blushed but responded anyway. “And I love it when you do.”

Doc scooted them with his hands. “Okay, folks. I’m done with you.”

“What do I owe you, Doc?”

“For the removal of the bullet and the stitches, it’s

three dollars. The removal of said stitches today is included."

"I never got around to paying you when we came in, so here's a five." Jared pulled a gold piece from his pocket. "Keep the change and thanks for carrying me. Who pays you for treating Stockton's injuries? Me or the courts?"

"Probably the courts whenever they get around to it. But I don't care if I never get paid…it was worth it to see him in the same shape he'd left the girls he was with." Doc grinned. .

She faced the doctor. "Thanks for everything, Doc. I know I'm alive because of you so anything you need let me know."

"I've already been paid and that's enough. Maybe you can make us a pie. The missus, doesn't bake very well. We for the most part have gotten used to going without dessert."

Angelica smiled. "I'd be happy to. Whenever I bake desserts, I'll make you one. It will be my pleasure because I do love to bake."

Jared patted his belly. "I can attest that she's a wonderful baker. I'm almost out of pants because I'm gaining weight."

She laughed. "Don't you believe him, Doc. I doubt he's gained a pound, despite my desserts every night."

Doc smiled and shook his head. "Well, thank you. Mabel and I will enjoy them I'm sure. Now I probably have other patients to see, so I'll say goodbye until you bring over a pie."

Jared took Angelica's hand. "See you later, Doc."

"Yes and thank you. I'll be over later with that pie. Do you want me to bring it here or your apartment upstairs?"

"Here is fine. Mabel will take it up."

Jared headed out the door holding her hand until they were outside. Then he put his arms around her and brought her close. "I love touching you, even if it's just scratching your shoulder."

She wrapped her arms around his neck. "And I you. But we are being scandalous…touching…even kissing…in public."

"I don't care who knows I love my wife."

"And I love my husband."

He took her lips with his and kissed her.

She kissed him back putting all the love in her heart in the kiss.

"Shall we go home? Then I have to go to work and walk my rounds. Also, make sure Stockton is not comfortable. I told Bill to do what he wanted to make Clay as miserable as possible."

She chuckled. "I'll bet Bill came up with something good."

"We'll see."

Jared took her hand and walked her the rest of the way home, taking his leave after he dropped her at the door with another toe-curling kiss.

She opened the door and went into the living room.

"I was hoping Jared would come in with you."

Angelica screamed. Her pulse racing, she whirled around, hearing the sneering voice behind her. *I should have known something was wrong when the door was unlocked.* "Clay. How did you get here? You should be in jail."

"That moron Jared had guarding me unlocked the door to give me my dinner. I took advantage and slammed the door open with all my strength, which is still considerable despite the beating Robbie gave me. The deputy was on the floor when I left."

Her heart pounded and she realized she might die. "When Jared sees you're gone this house is the first place he'll come looking for you. You're not safe here."

Clay stepped away from the far wall of the living room, a pistol leveled at her. "I know that, but I need provisions and a horse. You're getting them. Now, let's go."

"All right. Don't shoot me. I just got the stitches out from the last time you did."

He kept the gun leveled on her. "I never meant to shoot you then. I was aiming for Jared. But now is different. I'm desperate Angelica, so do as I say."

"All right." She went to the kitchen.

Clay followed her.

She walked directly to the icebox where she pulled out the roast beef from last night's dinner. Then she got a flour sack from the pantry and put the roast in it. Her hands shook so much she could barely wrap the last of the biscuits from breakfast in a piece of oil cloth and put them in the bag, too. "That's all I have prepared. It will have to do." She held out the bag toward him.

From the corner of her eye she could see out the kitchen window. Jared had his gun out and was headed toward the back door. She didn't do anything to acknowledge his presence.

Suddenly, the kitchen door flew open and Jared appeared, shooting Clay before he had a chance to turn toward him.

Clay was dead from the head wound before he hit the floor.

Angelica flew across the floor to Jared, tears rolling down her cheeks.

"Angel, are you hurt? Why are you crying?"

"I was so scared and then when I saw you out the window, I figured Clay did, too. But he didn't. And then his body crumpling to the floor. Oh, Jared, I've never been so scared in my life. I was so afraid he would shoot you and I couldn't bare it."

"Everything's all right now, Angel but I want the doctor to check you and make sure the baby is well."

She sniffled and then nodded. "I'm fine really. Now that you're here. I'm okay."

He pulled her close. "I'm sorry. Usually we don't have much happening in town besides bar brawls and things like that. Murderers generally leave town as soon as possible. What did Clay want?"

"He wanted provisions and a horse. I'd just given him the bag with the food that I had available."

"That was favorable timing. His attention was on you and I could shoot him before he shot me or you again."

She buried her face against Jared's chest. The sight of Clay's dead body turned her stomach. "Get me out of here. I don't want to see him anymore, even in death. I just want to stay with you."

He put his arms around her. "I know you do. But I have to leave to get Bill and Robbie."

Angelica looked up at him, clutching the front of his shirt. "Please, let me come with you. I can't stay in this house as long as he's there." She buried her face in Jared's chest.

He kissed the top of her head. "All right. Are you ready?"

"More than ready." She clutched at his hand. Angelica didn't feel safe without touching him. He was real. He saved her from being killed. She needed him more than ever.

"Let's go. Are you sure you don't need to see Doc?"

"Yes, I'm fine. Really fine…now, thanks to you."

Jared steered them out the back door and toward Robbie's house. He put his arm around her shoulders. "I'll always be here for you. I love you so much? Just the thought of being without you makes my heart ache."

She leaned into his side as they walked to Robbie's house. "I feel the same way. I don't know how or when, but I fell in love with you faster than I ever would have believed. I'm so glad I did and that you love me back." She put her free hand on her stomach. "This baby will live with two parents who love him and each other…forever."

Jared stopped walking and took her in his arms, kissing her. She felt the love radiating from him. "Forever."

EPILOGUE

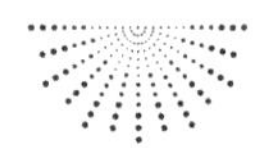

June 7, 1863, The Winslow home.

"Angel, don't you want to sit down? It can't be good for you to wear yourself out now… before the baby comes." Jared sat on the side of the bed and patted the place next to him.

"I'm fine," she barked then breathed out a long sigh and pressed the fingers of both hands on the small of her back. "I'm sorry, my love. I don't mean to snap at you."

He smiled and then stood and came to her. He tried to put his arms around her but needed to go to the side of her rounded stomach to do it. "I know you don't mean it, though, I admit it's hard to hear that tone coming from you. Doc warned me you'd say lots of things you don't mean, due to the pain."

Tears formed in her eyes. "It is. I would never say anything awful to you. I love you so very much. I just wish your son or daughter would hurry up and get here. Mama is already tired of this and it's only been a few hours. Doc said some women go through days of labor before finally delivering their babes."

Jared's face lost all color and turned pasty white, quite the contrast with his dark mustache.

Chuckling, she took his hand. "Don't worry, I don't believe I'll be in labor that long. I feel the baby moving. As a matter of fact, if Doc doesn't get here soon, *you* may have to deliver your child."

She didn't know how he did it but her husband became even paler.

He swallowed hard. "Me?! Deliver my baby? Oh, no." He shook his head vigorously. "I can't. No, not me."

Angelica laughed. "Don't worry, darlin'. I won't make you deliver your baby."

"I should say not." Doctor Schossow bustled into the room, followed by Rosie Johnson. "That's my job. Now, Jared, why don't you go let Rosie take care of you. She let me in by the way. Bill is down there with all the kids, too."

"Come on, Jared. I'll make you dinner," said Rosie, a tall, robust woman with dark black hair and a no nonsense attitude.

Jared shook his head. "I'm not leaving Angel."

Angelica smiled up at her husband and then moved her gaze to the doctor. "I'd like him to stay as long as he can."

The doctor furrowed his brows and pursed his lips. Then he sighed. "All right, but don't get in my way. As a matter of fact you stay at the head of the bed the whole time. You can hold her hands or something. Rosie will take care of the baby when it comes."

"Right now, I just want him to walk with me. Lord, I hurt."

Jared jumped up and went to Angelica. "Here, love, let me help." He put his arm around her waist and held her as she walked.

The doctor washed his hands in a basin Angelica had put on the commode for his use.

She'd also covered the top of the bureau with towels and another basin to clean the baby in, towels to dry him off, diapers and a soft little blanket to swaddle him.

Doctor Schossow dried his hands. "When did your water break?"

"Last night, so going on twenty-four hours now. I'm so ready to have this baby."

Jared kept his arm around her as she shuffled across the room, her gait getting slower and slower. "She's exhausted, Doc. Can't you do something?"

"This is Mother Nature's show. The only thing I can do is be here if something goes wrong and to catch the baby when it's right. Now. I need to look and see where you are. Lie down please, Angelica."

She waddled over to the bed, her hands still holding her back. When she sat, she whooshed out a breath and lay on her side. "Jared, help me lift my legs, please. I'm afraid if I put any pressure on my stomach, I'll have the baby. I can feel him coming."

He lifted her legs.

She rolled to her back.

Jared pulled over all the pillows, from the bed and the one he'd retrieved earlier from the sofa in the living room and piled them behind her back. "Is that better?"

Pain throbbed through her body as she gritted her teeth and nodded.

Doc sat on the foot of the bed. "All right, Angelica, pull your nightgown up around your waist and spread your knees wide. I want to see what's happening with your baby."

She lifted her gown and then raised her knees letting them fall wide to the sides.

"Well, it looks like you're correct. The baby is starting to crown. I need you to bear down as hard as you can. Push, Angelica. Push for your baby."

She pushed and the burning sensation threatened to make her stop, but she worried if she did now, the baby might die. So she pushed for all she was worth and then did it again.

Jared held his hands out to her.

She grasped them.

"That's right sweetheart. Take my hands and use me to push against. Squeeze my hands. You can't hurt me."

"All right," said Doctor Schossow. "Push again… harder…harder still. You can do it, Angel."

Suddenly, the burning feeling intensified and she felt her body give way to the head of the baby.

"That's wonderful. The head is out. Now we need the rest of the baby so push again. Come on, now. You can do it. Push…push…push for all you're worth."

She pushed and bore down as hard as she could. Finally, she felt the baby slide from her body.

She fell limp against the pillows, breathing hard and trying to catch her breath. "What do we have? A boy or a girl?"

Doc smiled up at her. "You have a beautiful baby girl with brown hair and dark eyes. Whether they are blue or brown, I don't yet know for sure. We'll just have to wait and see."

She held up her arms. "I want her. I want to hold her."

Jared leaned down and kissed her. "Let Rosie get her cleaned up first."

Angelica nodded, but her arms ached for her baby. "All right but hurry Rosie."

The doctor chuckled. "Always in a hurry to get them out and then to take them back." He handed the baby to Rosie and he proceeded to deliver the after birth.

She took the babe back to the bureau where she

washed and dressed her in the items Angelica had laid out.

The baby liked none of this treatment and cried.

The little squeaks she made were music to her mother's ears.

Apparently, to her father's as well, since he gave Angelica's hand a squeeze.

Rosie brought the babe to the bed. "Here you go. I'd say here's your sweet little girl, but this one will be a firecracker. Mark my words. Let me get you and the bed cleaned up."

Rosie washed Angelica, put a fresh nightgown on her, and changed the sheets.

"Now I'll get the family and take our leave. We'll be by to visit tomorrow or the next day."

Jared shook Rosie's hand with both of his. "Thank you for everything."

Angelica touched her daughters little button nose, ran her finger along her delicate brow and kissed her pink skin. She looked up from her daughter to her friend. "Thank you, Rosie."

Rosie smiled. "You're welcome." She shut the door gently as she left.

Jared walked to the doctor and shook his hand. "What do I owe you?"

"I'll put it on your bill. You three have a good evening together."

"We will, Thanks for everything, Doc."

"You're very welcome. Goodnight now." He picked

up his case with one hand and a bucket containing the afterbirth with the other.

"Goodnight." Jared walked back to the bed.

"Well, what do you think, Daddy?" She couldn't take her gaze off her daughter.

"I think she's as pretty as her mama."

She turned her face up. "Ah, you're so sweet. I must look a wreck."

Jared leaned down and kissed her. "You look beautiful, as always." He pushed a lock of hair behind her ear. "Thank you for my daughter and for coming into my life, giving me something I never thought I needed and now, couldn't do without."

Angelica smiled. "Love?"

He nodded. "Love."

"Now we have a new little someone to love. What shall we name her? Do you still agree on naming her after my mother? Maybe her middle name could be after your mother. What was her name?"

"Faye."

"That's it, Edwina Faye." She held the baby in her arms and then kissed her lips, her cheeks and her lips again. "I've got you, Edwina. Mama's got you and she'll never let you go. You'll always be my first born."

Edwina looked up at her, wide-eyed and sniffled.

Jared reached down and put his finger in her hand.

The baby gripped it.

"May I hold her?"

"Oh, of course. Why don't you lie in bed with us?"

"Good idea." He climbed into bed next to her and Edwina.

She placed their daughter in her daddy's arms and saw how completely captivated he looked. The look of complete adoration on his face

Angelica was content. Actually more than content. She was happy. She leaned against Jared's shoulder and touched her daughters bottom lip as she lay in her daddy's arms. Angelica…Angel…her heart felt near to bursting, She never thought she could be this happy.

Jared wrapped an arm around her and brought her closer, the baby in his lap.

They lay there, together, the three of them, her family…her life…forever.

ABOUT THE AUTHOR

Cynthia Woolf is an award-winning and best-selling author of forty-five historical western romance novels and six sci-fi romance novels, which she calls westerns in space. Along with these books she has also published four boxed sets of her books.

Cynthia loves writing and reading romance. Her first western romance Tame A Wild Heart was inspired by the story her mother told her of meeting Cynthia's father on a ranch in Creede, Colorado. Although Tame A Wild Heart takes place in Creede that is the only similarity between the stories. Her father was a cowboy not a bounty hunter and her mother was a nursemaid (called a nanny now) not the owner of the ranch.

Cynthia credits her wonderfully supportive husband Jim and her great critique partners for saving her sanity and allowing her to explore her creativity.

STAY CONNECTED!

Newsletter

Sign up for my newsletter and get a free book.

Follow Cindy

https://www.facebook.com/cindy.woolf.5
https://twitter.com/CynthiaWoolf
http://cynthiawoolf.com

ALSO BY CYNTHIA WOOLF

Bachelors and Babies

Carter

Cupids & Cowboys

Lanie

The Marshal's Mail Order Brides

The Carson City Bride

The Virginia City Bride

The Silver City Bride

Brides of Homestead Canyon/Montana Sky Series

Thorpe's Mail-Order Bride

Kissed by a Stranger

A Family for Christmas

Bride of Nevada

Genevieve

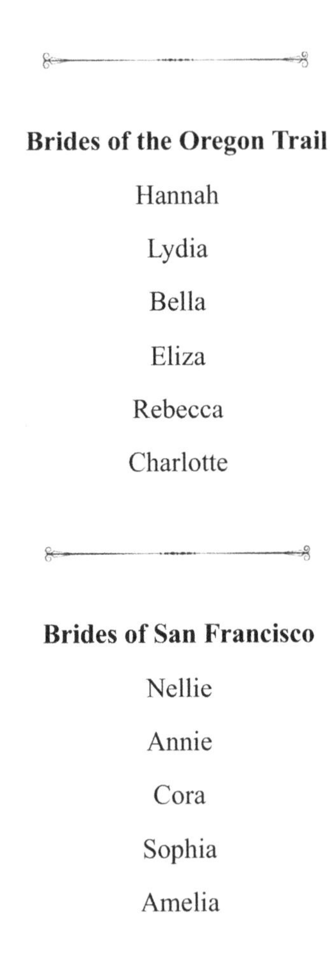

Brides of the Oregon Trail

Hannah

Lydia

Bella

Eliza

Rebecca

Charlotte

Brides of San Francisco

Nellie

Annie

Cora

Sophia

Amelia

Brides of Seattle

Mail Order Mystery

Mail Order Mayhem

Mail Order Mix-Up

Mail Order Moonlight

Mail Order Melody

Brides of Tombstone

Mail Order Outlaw

Mail Order Doctor

Mail Order Baron

Central City Brides

The Dancing Bride

The Sapphire Bride

The Irish Bride

The Pretender Bride

Destiny in Deadwood

Jake

Liam

Zach

Hope's Crossing

The Stolen Bride

The Hunter Bride

The Replacement Bride

The Unexpected Bride

Matchmaker & Co Series

Capital Bride

Heiress Bride

Fiery Bride

Colorado Bride

The Surprise Brides

Gideon

Tame

Tame a Wild Heart

Tame a Wild Wind

Tame a Wild Bride

Tame A Honeymoon Heart

Tame Boxset

Centauri Series (SciFi Romance)

Centauri Dawn

Centauri Twilight

Centauri Midnight

Singles

Sweetwater Springs Christmas

Made in the USA
Columbia, SC
22 January 2023

10774411R00104